Wendy S

Wendy Steele lives on a hillside in Wales. She can see the mountains from a place on her land where one day, she'll build a straw bale writing room.

She worked in the City, BC (Before Children) but since 1999 has indulged her creative side, training in natural therapies, belly dance and writing, culminating in her first novel, 'Destiny of Angels - First book in the Lilith Trilogy' and in 2012, her first non-fiction title ' Wendy Woo's Year - A Pocketful of Smiles'.

Wendy is passionate about writing magical realism, bringing real people and real magic to her readers. The Standing Stone Series are the latest books in this genre, linking three women across time and space with the goddesses who can inspire them.

Wendy lives with her partner, Mike, and four cats. When not writing or teaching dance, she spends her days renovating her house, clearing her land and, when time and weather allows, sitting on her riverbank, breathing in the beauty of nature.

Also by Wendy Steele

Fiction

Destiny of Angels
First Book in The Lilith Trilogy

Wrath of Angels
Second Book in The Lilith Trilogy

Too Hot for Angels
Six (eXtra Sexy) Extended Scenes
(The Lilith Trilogy)

Turn Down The Heat
A Short Story Anthology

Into The Flames
A Short Story Anthology

The Standing Stone - Home For Christmas
First Novella in The Standing Stone Series

The Standing Stone – Silence Is Broken
Second Novella in The Standing Stone Series

Non-Fiction

Wendy Woo's Year - A Pocketful of Smiles
101 ideas for a happy year and a happy you

The Standing Stone

The Gathering

Wendy Steele

PHOENIX &
THE DRAGON

www.wendysteele.com

Text Copyright © Wendy Steele 2016
Published 2016, in Great Britain,
by Phoenix & The Dragon

All rights reserved. No part of this publication may be reproduced, stored in a retrieval system, or transmitted in any form or by any means, electronic, mechanical, photocopy, recording or otherwise, without prior written permission of the copyright owner. Nor can it be circulated in any form of binding or cover other than that in which it is published and without similar condition including this condition being imposed on a subsequent purchaser.

Please visit www.wendysteele.com
for contact details

ISBN 978-1533227522

British Cataloguing Publication data:
A catalogue record of this book is available from
the British Library

This book is also available as an ebook
Please visit
www.wendysteele.com
for more details.

This book is dedicated to the women I've met since I arrived in Wales

Beautiful, inspiring and loving, you make my life

Home

Think of me in this barren landscape
Think of me, on this hill
Far away from love and friendship
Think of me, if you will.

Spare a tear for my weighty burden
Digging new this foreign land
Felling trees to build my homestead.
Hearth and home made with this hand.

But the earth, it is the same earth
And the sea 'tween shore and shore
Gives me hope in times of hardship
That I'm coming home once more.
Coming home, I'm coming home
Coming home from distant shore.

Think of me as I bring in the harvest
Plucking crop from land and tree
Tending flock and growing family
Dry your eyes and think of me.

Trees and hilltops, plants and flowers
Glossy stars that light Her dome
Where I live in Nature's beauty
That to me, is truly home.

But the earth, it is the same earth
And the sea 'tween shore and shore
Gives me hope in times of hardship
That I'm coming home once more.
Coming home, I'm coming home
Coming home from distant shore.

Chapter 1

As she lay in the bath, a face rose unbidden in her mind. The face became a man and Oliver stood, naked to the waist, his torso tanned and chiselled and his hazel green eyes twinkling with desire. As she watched he became clothed in a tuxedo, holding out his arm as she descended a curving staircase in a flowing turquoise gown. Out of the bath she smiled at her reflection as she pulled on her jeans and jumper. She waited, impatiently, for Rhys, glad when she heard the familiar tyres on the drive. She opened the door to greet him and was shocked to see him attired in a belted green shift, grey trousers and a cloak held with a sculpted metal pin. He held a staff in one hand, with a large milky crystal set into the top and a wicker basket on his arm covered by a cloth. His dreadlocks were adorned with beads, shells and bells. She held a hand to her mouth, stifling a laugh.

"Are you ready?" asked Rhys, blushing under her stare. "Have you a lantern?"

Rachel ran indoors, glad to get away, giggling as she found her lantern and spare candles. "Why are you dressed like that?" she asked as they set off for the mound.

"These are special clothes for a special occasion," said Rhys, "Why so funny?"

"Not funny, just not what I expected, that's all."

Rhys stopped and looked at her, the lantern light adding sharp lines to his already angular face. He looked about to speak but shook his head and walked on. As they neared the mound and the path wove through the trees, Rhys began to sing, touching the trees with his staff. Rachel muffled her laughter with her hand. Climbing the mound, Rhys bowed to the standing stone before walking around the circle. He placed stones around the edge and set out his cloth before the stone.

"Can I just watch?" asked Rachel, kneeling beside Rhys at the cloth to lend him her light.

"No," said Rhys.

"Oh."

"You can take part or you can go home."

"Why are you being like this?"

"I'm not being anything, Rachel. You can laugh at me and what I'm wearing, but you can't be disrespectful here."

"You've a bloody cheek!" cried Rachel, standing up. "This is my land, I'll do what I like!"

"Shall I leave?" asked Rhys.

"Please yourself," said Rachel, "but I'm not staying here to be insulted any more!"

She turned to leave.

"Why can't you see what's before your eyes?" called Rhys, "The Land will help you, heal you and support you if you let it. It's part of you!"

Rachel hurried down the path, hot tears burning her eyes.

After an hour of sobbing, she heard his van start up and back slowly down her drive. She threw the cushion she'd been hugging onto the floor making Angel Face leap off the sofa and hide beneath it. His scared face, peeping from underneath did nothing to dissuade her as she screamed through the house, throwing crockery and books and clearing surfaces with a swipe of her arm. In less than five minutes, the cottage was trashed and with her energy gone, she sat on the floor among the debris and wept.

As a chill descended on the house, she realised there was no firewood so she slipped on the nearest coat and hurried outside to fetch it. Once indoors with the burner blazing she flung her coat on the sofa where it rolled over tumbling a black and white shiny card onto the floor.

"Hello? Is that Oliver? Hi, it's Rachel. How are you?"

"Rachel! What a lovely surprise!"

"I found your card in my pocket and wondered how you were doing."

"I'm good. I'm staying with Beth and Alan while my house is being refurbished. How are you?"

"Not bad," said Rachel, surveying the destruction around her. "Been enjoying the garden."

"We've been lucky with the weather though Beth says it won't last. Her witches nose tells her there is rain coming or something!"

"Women's intuition?"

"Or reading too many folk tales! I'm not a gardener myself. Happy to sit in it but prefer to pay someone else to look after it."

"The garden keeps me busy."

"I'm glad. I've been worrying about you."

"Me? Why?"

"Because I was an idiot at Beth's birthday and I was worried I had upset you."

"I was fine...am fine, in fact. Let's not talk about me. Where's your new house?"

"Just outside town, on the road to the coast. I'm going down tomorrow to check the plastering before the kitchen is fitted. Come with me."

"I...well..."

"I'll pick you up at 2pm. It's just a drive out."

"Thanks, Oliver but..."

"I'll let you treat me to ice cream at Aberaeron after."

Rachel smiled. She couldn't help herself. His persistence amused her. "Okay, thanks."

"Great! I'll see you at 2pm. Wait! Your address?"

"Beth knows where I am."

"I'll ask her now. See you tomorrow. It'll be fun."

"Looking forward to it."

She meant the words as she spoke them but once she'd hung up the phone and looked at the mess at her feet, she wished she'd been firmer. As she started picking up her books, a warm glow began in the pit of her stomach. She needed to clear up anyway and what harm was there in going for a drive with a handsome man?

As the half moon appeared hazy in the dark cloudy sky, Candy sat at the fire she had made in a rusting cauldron. From the shelves inside the cottage she had retrieved a number of tins. Once the rusty tin opener had been mastered, the third tin produced a creamy chicken soup. Heated in the embers, she ate it with a bent spoon. The

The Standing Stone – The Gathering

warm satisfying meal dispelled her fear and sadness and as she looked up at the moon, hope began to return. Plans developed in her head as she tucked into tinned peaches, drinking the juice from the can as if it were life giving elixir.

She talked to the moon about the cottage and the people in it until the fire went out. In the barn, Candy settled into her straw bed, lulled to sleep by the baas of sheep, an owl calling and the tinkle of gentle rain on the rusty tin roof.

Days turned to weeks as Candy made her home. She swept first, from floor to ceiling, clouds of dust and dirt billowing around her. Carrying up water from the river, she washed the tiny windows and mopped the lime washed stone walls, allowing some sunlight to pervade. Caught up in this domestic bliss, Candy realised she was no longer counting her beats. As she busied around the house, clearing out cupboards, often thanking the previous occupants out loud, there was no need to check if she was still alive.

A trunk at the end of the bed held a multitude of cloth and woollen items and soon the cottage was decked in bright yellow and white checked curtains and she, in denim dungarees and a pink jumper which hung to her knees. The sheep grew braver, following her on her trips to the river. In a cupboard in the barn, she found salt licks, which endeared her to them even more.

Beyond the small back garden, Candy recovered the remains of a vegetable plot and green house from the choking weeds. She used her mattock to break open the soil and was soon joined by a vocal robin and a bossy blackbird. A large square tin in the kitchen revealed open, grubby looking seed packets which she diligently sewed and watered in her greenhouse, calling upon the goddess to give strength to her new plants. Further inspection behind the greenhouse revealed a pump, rusty and immobile but with a thick raspy file and some smelly oil, the pump worked, dispensing with the time consuming job of bringing water from the river.

Some days, as she worked in her greenhouse or sat talking to the sheep, she thought of the village and Ben and Artie but mainly she thought of the future and the prospect of making her home right here and one day, maybe, setting off to see if she had neighbours.

Late one sunny afternoon, Candy lay naked in the tin bath in front of the barn. Two lambs, Fluff and Cloud, now almost sheep, head butted each other in tumbling, noisy play and she watched them, laughing at their antics. A baa, followed by another came from the river. She turned towards the noise and saw more sheep and a man dressed in khaki with a rucksack on his back.

She rose from the bath, wrapping her towel around her and preparing to run.

"Wait, Candy!" he cried, "It's me!"

The Whisperer had found her.

She stood immobile, feet and legs chilling in the water as Aaron approached, followed by a crowd of nosy sheep and lambs. Her towel flapped in the breeze and she ran into the barn before Aaron reached her and emerged, fully dressed and wielding a shot gun.

The Standing Stone – The Gathering

"Woah!" said Aaron, raising his hands and stopping beside the tin bath.

"What are you doing here?"

"Some welcome, Candy! I came to find you!"

"But how...who sent you?"

"Can't we go in?" Aaron nodded towards the house but kept his arms aloft.

"No, I'll light a fire and you can tell me why you are here."

She lowered the shot gun, putting on the safety catch and worked on her fire. The last time she had seen Aaron was on the Screen beside Abraham Adams Manager 37 as she was accused of disobeying a Lesson. The last time she had heard his voice was as a whisper of hope as the table she was clamped to after being found guilty, began its journey out of the Dome before dropping her in the river.

"They found out I helped you," said Aaron, shaking his head, "Caught me leaving your interrogation room."

"What happened?"

"I was subjected to the same treatment as you."

"But you can see."

Aaron had tied something around her eyes to prevent the laser blinding her.

He laughed and lay down on the earth by the fire. "Having AAM37 as my birth father has some compensations!"

"Your father?"

"I'm afraid so but at least I tried and I know most of those I helped survived."

"How do you know?"

"Anna. She found me by the pool."

Candy put larger branches on top of her kindling sending sparks crackling skyward. The sun had dropped behind the hills in a cloudless sky. Night fell crisp and cold.

"Did you save Paul?"

"Paul?

"My guard partner."

Candy opened two precious tins and poured the thick creamy soup into her cooking pot.

"I didn't see him in the interrogation rooms."

"What does that mean?"

"It wasn't my job, Candy. I'm a scientist, a human biologist. I was tolerated by my father. He was proud of my academic achievements and thought my interest in the people under interrogation was for part of my work. Well, I let him believe that but I couldn't be there for every interrogation."

Candy nodded. She poked her fire, red hot embers glistening like jewels in the centre, before carefully arranging five small logs over the coals. "It doesn't explain why you came here."

"You disappeared, Candy. They were worried."

Candy leaned behind her and picked up the shot gun. She flicked off the safety catch and pointed the gun at Aaron. "One more lie and you join the corpses in the garden."

The Standing Stone – The Gathering

Excitement grew as the villagers prepared for the evening. They decorated rings of twisted willow with flowers and leaves and Mara sat with a crowd around her, painting flowers on faces. As the sun began to drop in the sky, three tribes gathered to proceed to the mound, led by young men carrying flaming torches. They called ahead to the spirits of the Land that the people were bringing offerings and blessings to the Standing Stone.

A slow drum beat settled the crowd encircling the Standing Stone as Nia and Fern stepped towards it.

"Great Mother, Goddess of this fertile Land, we welcome you! You hold the balance in your hands, of dark and light, night and day and we say 'Bring in the light!'" cried Nia.

"Bring in the light!" echoed the villagers.

"The dark days are behind us and we look forward to the light! We honour and beseech you, great Mother, to look kindly on your people," said Fern, "Our village has grown. Dark times have led others in need of shelter to this place, and we all, as one, come to show our love and respect for you."

Fern broke a precious chicken egg and dripped its contents on the ground while Nia held up a stoppered clay jar.

"It is the time when the day and night are balanced in your hands, great Mother." She drizzled mead from the jar onto the grass. "Bring us long days of sunshine to aid our work and make our crops grow."

"We call upon the faerie folk and the spirits of the Land," said Fern, "To bear witness to the commitment we make to plough the soil, plant new trees and tend to the abundance in the hedgerows. We hear the birds of the air and the animals of the Land and we echo their excitement as you bring the light."

Nia picked up her besom and held it aloft. "Before you all, I sweep away the darkness, the dark thoughts and the dark deeds, leaving room in our lives and hearts for the blessings of Spring."

Around the central fire, the villagers danced to the drums and shared their ritual feast before Mara stood and gestured for quiet.

"I thank you on behalf of my people for your welcome and acceptance of our tribe. Nia, Fern, Adalbern, please accept these gifts as tokens of our friendship and know, though we are Boat People, our commitment to peace on this precious Land is the same as yours."

Three rings of hammered gold were given, the villagers gasping and shrieking with wonder at the sparkling metal, the colour of warm honey, as it reflected and refracted light from the fire. Fern saw envious looks on faces.

"Thank you, Mara for these beautiful gifts. I shall treasure my ring as a symbol of friendship between our tribes as we endeavour to live in harmony with the Land and the other people upon it."

As the first trunk began to take on a boat-like shape, Fern convinced herself that seeking trees further down river was the right thing to do. Defending the village had become a priority but what of the weaving house and tending to the fields and animals? Were there enough people to ensure a good harvest to support the village in the coming months?

First Adalbern and his followers had joined her village and now Mara and her people had sought refuge and a new life for themselves. Warriors had attacked two villages now and the necessity to defend themselves had forced the decision to cut more trees from their precious Land. And this wouldn't be the end as more trees to the east, alongside Adalbern's long house, would need to be cleared to plant more crops. Felling and moving trees took time and Fern felt ill equipped to decide whether to defend or feed the growing village. Seed had been planted in the usual fields but this would not sustain them all. Fishing and hunting parties needed to be organised so fish and meat could be dried and salted, which reminded her that it was less than two moon cycles until the Gathering. No time had been set aside to made goods to barter for precious salt, cloth and seed.

The Gathering was the place where all the neighbouring tribes came together, welcoming traders from far away to barter with and exchange news and stories. Two days of excitement after a long walk, culminated in lighting the Midsummer fire and thanking the gods and goddesses for the green and fertile Land upon which they lived. From the Gathering on top of the hill, other fires could be seen, burning brightly, flames spiralling into the sky and illuminating the sacred circle and avenue and casting shadows at the temple entrance.

Fern loved the Gathering but she was worried that the village was unprepared. Could the villagers leave their houses to the Olds and few adults who remained behind? What if the warriors attacked?

Fern went to find Nia. Change had brought fear to their peaceful village and she sometimes wished that everything could stay the same. Nia was in their house, rocking a baby by the fire. The mother, one of Mara's people, had been taken by a fever but the baby was healthy, taking milk from another mother.

Fern voiced her concerns to Nia as she lay the baby in the woven basket, beside the child she would call sister.

"You are right," said Nia, "The Boat people men build the boats and their few women, apart from Mara, are busy with babies. It is up to us to find those to hunt and assemble our goods for barter. I will speak to Agnes about woven goods."

"And I'll speak to Adalwin about men to expand our field area."

"That leaves hunting."

"Leave that to me. I've an idea about that."

"As you wish," said Nia, bowing to her.

"Stop it," said Fern, "We're working together, remember."

Nia had taken care of Fern and her younger sister, Rowan ever since their mother had died. She had also taken on Fern's mother's role as wise woman of the village, bringing Council together to discuss village matters and advising on how to proceed but after the Midwinter ritual at the Standing Stone, when Fern had

The Standing Stone – The Gathering

travelled across time and space to join Rachel and Candy, two other travellers, Nia had treated her differently. Though the villagers had only seen her face transform and the words of her song uplift them, they believed Fern to be a goddess or a spirit of the Land, once human but now blessed by the gods. Fern learned of her mother's lineage but felt inadequate to take on her role so asked Nia if they could continue advising and learning together.

"I'm teasing. Did you see, the children have begun digging the ditch?" Nia's tired eyes sparkled with mischief.

"I know! I saw them when I was on guard duty. The fact the village sits atop a slope is a help but the hole they have dug so far wouldn't stop a rabbit!"

"But they are occupied, as we must keep the men."

Fern shivered and drew nearer to the fire. The cold damp day had chilled her but her mind dissected Nia's words and she understood. "To keep their minds from warfare."

"You learn quickly."

When the first threat to their village had come, when the hairy stranger brought news of warriors murdering his village, Fern had instigated an ongoing routine of making bows and arrows and teaching those able, to shoot a bow. Much gesturing and posturing with swords had followed but the rigours of daily survival had lessened the men's cries for blood.

With a skin over her head against a sudden down pour, Fern found her companions, Sky and River, making bread. They gladly followed Fern, though the other women grumbled, and they ran laughing together under the skin to Adalbern's house.

Dark and noisy within, the men had abandoned outdoor tasks in favour of a hot meal, so Fern scoured the floor and benches for Adalwin. She turned to her name and a raised hand drew her to the man who, though of a different tribe, she loved with a desire that burned her. She blushed and smiled as she, Sky and River sat beside him. Fern looked around for Geirr, Adalbern's spiritual guide and translator, and once he arrived, explained her idea to Adalwin.

"All three of us can use a bow and Mara has showed us how to catch fish with a spear," said Fern. "With three more practised hunters with us, we can double the amount of meat and fish being brought into the village."

"Fishing, maybe," said Adalwin, "But hunting, especially at this time of year when the prey have offspring, is too dangerous."

"Then train us so we are prepared for danger. In your village and mine, men only teach the boys to hunt."

"Some girls want to do more than rock babies, make bread and stir broth," grinned Sky.

"And some of us are more than capable," insisted River.

Adalwin smiled at their eager faces. Fern tucked her hands beneath her and sat on them, fearing she would grab his gentle face and kiss him. Time alone together was rare and she longed for another night losing herself in his arms.

The Standing Stone – The Gathering

"Men are needed to clear trees for the new field so less will be available to hunt," insisted Fern, "If we start now and continue after the Gathering, no one will go hungry this winter."

Adalwin nodded, his smooth brow furrowing until he reached a decision. "If Mara's men will include you on their fishing parties, we will train you in our hunt. When the boats are ready and return with trees for our defences, many men will be busy. Maybe this is the right time to invest in increasing our food supplies."

"You do not have to make this decision alone. All tribes should work together before and after the Gathering. Nia will call Council. I wanted to make sure you would support my words."

Chapter 2

It was the briefest of notes. Rhys had called to see her and hoped she was okay. Rachel opened the door of the wood burner to incinerate his note and growled at the dull grey ash within. Lighting a fire as her only source of heat annoyed her. Rhys had discovered the immersion heater switch so hot water was no longer a problem but splitting and barrowing wood had lost its novelty. Rhys' absence after their argument on the mound at the Spring Equinox meant fending for herself. She didn't need his help or advice. She would use the immersion heater as much as she wanted. With money landing in her account every week, she didn't care about the cost. Marcus had left her to manage alone so his money could pay her bills.

As she climbed into her boots, tears filled her eyes but she wiped them away with disgust. Alone on her hilltop she would not cry for the husband who took his own life and abandoned her or for the man she had called friend who lived in a cow shed and thought she could find answers to her life by communing with the land.

The second barrow was the last of the wood from the wood store so she telephoned the number on her pad by the phone and scheduled a delivery for Saturday morning. There was wood in the drying barn but it would need a chain saw before she could think about splitting it. She would order her wood ready chopped and split.

As the kindling caught and the room began to warm, she sat on the sofa with Merlin, Sphinx like behind her, looking out of the window as Angel Face crept in from the kitchen. Rhys had fitted a cat flat for him so the little feral kitten had begun to make himself at home. After last night's fracas, Angel Face sat on the rug in front of the fire and began his washing routine.

She'd enjoyed her day out; Oliver's house was beautiful. Detached and off the road by a short track, the house had new flat walls, new wooden floors throughout the downstairs and a master bedroom big enough for a four poster bed. Viewing the plans for the kitchen with its glass extension that eased out into the garden, she declared it a glorious room to have breakfast in. Set in an acre, the house and gardens were peaceful and secluded and Oliver had plans to convert a barn to one side of the land into a 'cinema come games room'.

"I know it's a long way from the house but with my popcorn and beer under my arm, it'll be like going to the movies."

She had laughed, in fact she had a fun afternoon while Oliver showed off his house and grew excited talking about his plans. One of the other bedrooms upstairs was to be his office, miles of cabling having already been threaded between the walls, while he planned a walk in shower room in his en suite and an outdoor hot tub area on the other side to the conservatory.

Rachel sipped her tea as she watched Angel Face washing, licking a paw before wiping it behind his ear for the twentieth time. Oliver knew what he wanted. He wasn't afraid to say either as she had hurried outside while he argued with the builder and electrician that the inset ceiling lights were not exactly down the middle of the hallway. He was different when he retrieved her from the garden with an apology. Relaxed, they had driven to the coast and sat on the wind swept stones at Aberaeron, eating honey ice cream. She liked him in a jeans and sweater though she noticed a designer label on both.

Loading the wood burner disturbed Angel Face, who ran to the doorway before turning and looking at her. She sat back on the sofa and beckoned him over but the little kitten shunned the invitation and resumed his perch by the fire.

Rachel recognised the familiar stomach flip followed by heat rising through her before the inevitable tears prickled her eyes. The future lay ahead of her but where to begin? She had alleviated one daily worry, keeping warm, by ordering logs but what to do with the rest of her life was a much bigger dilemma. Owning her own hair salon no longer seemed important and Ffion had said she was welcome to work at the salon, if she wanted some company. With Marcus' vast inheritance now passed to her, she could do anything but overwhelmed with such responsibility, she did nothing. She needed a focus, something she could put her mind to in the near future. She needed a goal to work towards.

The following day she met Beth in the coffee shop in the health food shop in town.

The Standing Stone – The Gathering

"I'm so glad Ffion's happy and she and the baby are well," said Rachel.

"You should go and see her," said Beth, sipping at her hot chocolate.

"I will."

Though over two years had passed since the loss of her baby, she shuddered as the familiar emotions overwhelmed her.

"You cold? Drink your hot chocolate."

"No, just memories, I'm fine."

"You're very pale, you sure?"

Telling Oliver that her husband had died on Christmas Eve had seemed difficult but this was even harder. She had told no one about baby Jack and she wasn't sure if she wanted to. She remembered Beth's kindness on Christmas Day and took a deep breath.

"Two years ago, I had a baby. His name was Jack and he was stillborn."

"Oh Rachel, I'm so sorry. I had no idea and there's me going on about Ffion's baby."

Rachel took a sip from her mug and the warm, creamy chocolate sustained her. "Life goes on, Beth, it's okay. I'm happy for Ffion and of course I will visit her."

"I'd understand if you didn't."

"I'm learning to face the world again. Coming to meet you today was a big deal for me but I'm here."

"Small steps sounds a good plan."

Rachel thought of the lantern that the Great Mother, Binah had given her and nodded. "But right now, I need a project, something to do that's useful and worthwhile. I'm sick of logs and weeds!"

Beth laughed. "I know that feeling. Well, I'm organising an event for Midsummer's Day to be held in the grounds of the University."

"Really? Tell me."

"Ffion's baby was healthy as you know but, if he'd needed an incubator, the hospital only has one and there was already a poorly baby in it so, she and I decided to start raising money for another one."

"Can I help?"

"Of course but are you sure? Isn't this a bit, well, close to home?"

"Maybe this is what I need," said Rachel, her cheeks reddening, "Nothing could have saved Jack but the thought we could help save another baby is a positive way to remember him."

Beth leaned over the table and squeezed Rachel's hand. "I think that's a great idea."

"So tell me what you're planning and what I can do to help."

"It was Artie more than anyone," said Aaron, raising his hands, "I shouldn't have lied, I'm sorry."

"Then why say they all missed me?"

Aaron shrugged. Candy replaced the safety catch and laid the gun beside her.

She resumed stirring her soup. "What did Artie say to you?"

The Standing Stone – The Gathering

"That he was worried. Worried you had gone to the Badland."

"Why would I do that?"

"He told me about the blacksmith...and the Partnering."

"So you've come to take me back to Three Oaks to be raped?"

Aaron shook his head. "No, I'm sorry about that and so's Artie."

"But he didn't warn me or try to stop them! Have you any idea how I felt, bound to a repulsive, stinking idiot and forced to lay with him?"

Aaron hung his head. "I'm sorry but the villages have rules..."

"And who makes the rules?"

Candy lifted the soup off the fire, poured it into two bowls and gave one to Aaron with a spoon.

"Thank you. Many people make the rules..."

"How are they chosen?"

"I don't know."

They ate their soup and Candy built up the fire.

"The man...did you...I mean..."

"I did what I had to do to escape but no woman should be forced to take a partner!"

"The villages must continue to grow so they need more children."

"You condone this barbaric practice?"

"No, but the Elders must have thought it for the best."

"Exactly. Nothing has changed and that's why I left."

"What do you mean?"

"Within the Dome, we work and we abide by the Lessons for the good of All and here, I was Partnered for the good of the villages. I choose freedom, Aaron. I make my own decisions here."

"What are you going to do?"

"Live here."

"How?"

"The Land will provide."

"On your own?"

"If necessary but soon, I'm going to walk and see if I have neighbours."

"But it's dangerous."

"Why?"

"This is the Badland."

"You're here."

They finished their soup in silence. The villagers of Three Oaks believed they were the furthest outpost of civilisation and that the land beyond them, the Badland, was their buffer to the sickness borne on the wind. The scientists at Three Elms monitored the air, Ben had told her, to make sure the sickness was not spreading but Candy knew the dead man in the cottage had been old and with the sheep thriving and her seeds growing, she saw no sickness in the Badland.

Candy poked her fire and put on more wood before hanging a pot of water over the flames. "Petty, small minded and selfish."

"Who?"

The Standing Stone – The Gathering

"The villagers. No one cares if there's people needing help out there." She gestured to the hills beyond the house.

"And you do?"

"Of course! I lived and worked for the good of All inside the Dome. It was a false reality engineered by others and I'm not sure exactly why yet. I do know that now I'm free, I must help others living outside."

"How? How can you help them?"

Candy shook her head. "I don't know but I must. Before Anna betrayed me, she said the plants I brought were useful and that my coming was a blessing. Did she tell you about that?"

"I saw the plants, yes and you are a blessing. That's why I've come, to take you home."

"Back to Three Oaks? No Aaron, I'm not going back."

"But Ben and Artie..."

"Were kind and I liked living with them but there is more for me to do."

"How do you know?"

Candy smiled. "I know. The Great Mother Binah told me there was another, a force to my form and the Goddess Ishtar told me I would need to be strong and fight for the people of the earth. That is my true path."

"You met these goddesses?"

"I did."

"But what will you do? How can you help people while you're living on your own out here? Come back to the village and the Elders can find you a new role, if you want to help."

"It won't happen," said Candy, "but you could stay."
"Stay with you?"
"Yes, or make a home of your own."

She watched his face in the firelight, dirty from his journey but animated by the possibility of a different future. She busied herself making drinks, spooning precious granules into two earthenware mugs. She thanked the owners of her cottage as she poured in the water. A tantalizing aroma tickled her nose as she passed a mug to Aaron.

"Have a cup of coffee while you think about it."

The rain eased, a watery sun shining through the clouds, steam to rising off the roofs of the houses. Nia called Council and they packed into the round house. Mara sat beside Fern, her decorated body covered by her cloak as Geirr translated Nia's words for his lord Adalbern and his followers. With Geirr's help, two men from each tribe became a working group of six whose tasks would be rotated every two days. Some of the younger boys and girls were allocated guard duty while Fern, Sky and River and three young men were to work with the hunting parties. Agnes and three other women from Adalbern's tribe were weaving cloth for barter and they would teach Nia and three more women. Belle's work with the chickens had produced many chicks so, half of these could go to the Gathering but there was a shortfall of goods for Fern's other plan.

She stood, clasping her hands in front of her as she explained her idea to the Council. "Change has come to

The Standing Stone – The Gathering

our village without our seeking it. Our village has grown and we must change to support ourselves. As we have discussed, more young people are joining the hunting parties but, in the future, this may still not be enough to feed us. We manage a few animals but my plan is to raise and rear sheep on a much bigger scale, giving us plenty of fleeces for wool, meat to eat and lambs to barter. Our children will learn shepherding with a dog and the Land will give us food to feed more sheep."

Some of the Olds nodded as Fern spoke and Geirr translated, while others seemed confused. The villagers near the doorway began to shout and comment until Nia stood and they fell silent.

"One at a time."

Belle and her husband took a few paces forward. "It takes time to birth the lambs and get them suckling," said Belle, "Sometimes, I'm up all night."

"Some die," said Aled, "and we don't know why."

"There are shepherds at the Gathering," said Fern, "We will ask and trade for advice."

"What with?" cried a voice from the doorway, "We have little enough to barter with for the salt we need!"

"Livestock costs much to buy and keep! If they get sick, we've wasted our time and we'll all go hungry!"

"Who wants to watch sheep in weather like this!"

Shouting rose in the Council hut once more until, to Fern's surprise, Geirr stood and addressed the villagers.

"You know I have travelled," said Geirr, rubbing his big red ears protruding from his felt hat, "and I was a shepherd in my youth. I know the ways of sheep and with tending, Fern is right. Using the grass on the hills around us is a good way to provide food and warmth for the village. I trained two dogs and can do it again."

"But how will we buy the sheep and rams? What will we barter with?" said Belle.

A hum began in the doorway, spreading out to a word by the time it reached Fern's ears.

"Gold." All the villagers stared at Mara.

"No," said Fern, "Our rings are gifts, precious and binding, bringing our tribes together as one village. We will find other goods to barter."

As Geirr translated, lord Adalbern, Adalwin's father stood and all around him sat quietly, awaiting his words.

"Fern thinks of the future of the village, three tribes working as one. Mara's people have joined us, bestowing gifts," he said, nodding and smiling at Mara, "and now I, Adalbern, wish to seal the union of three tribes in my way. Within the boat that brought us to this land, I carried my people with the skills we had but little else of value, save our children. The land we left behind was plundered for trees and stripped bare while men called themselves lords and judged their worth by the numbers of warriors who killed for them. With Nia's guidance and Fern's persuasion, I see that war is not always the answer."

He paused and spoke to Mara. "I would have killed you and your people and I am sorry."

From his belt he unstrapped a short scabbard from which he withdrew a dagger, decorated on the hilt with red, yellow and milky white stones. Gasps of wonder

The Standing Stone – The Gathering

rose from the villagers as Adalbern showed the dagger to them all.

"I will defend our village with sword and bow but this dagger shall buy sheep to feed us all!"

The villagers cheered and shouts of 'Adalbern' rang out. Fern turned to see Adalbern raising Mara to her feet and drawing her towards Adalwin.

Nia stood and gave news of the health of the babies and organised children for the morning to help her drag the small branches from the river to dry in the round houses for kindling but Fern heard little of it as she watched Adalbern, with Geirr translating, holding Mara's hand and Adalwin's. As they looked into each other's eyes, hot nausea rose from Fern's stomach. She turned away, tears rising. Once Council was over, she ran through the light rain falling from a pale blue sky, towards the mound and the Standing Stone.

Chapter 3

Oliver's rap on the front door roused her from the kitchen table. She stretched her arms above her head and rubbed her neck as she opened the door.

"Sorry, I didn't see the time. Have a seat and I'll be with you in a mo."

She changed her sweater for a short dress and her jeans for leggings before running a brush through her hair, mascara through her lashes and adding a smudge of lip gloss to her lips. She came down to put her boots on to find Oliver in the kitchen.

"What's all this?" he said, glaring at Rachel, his nostrils flaring.

Rachel's kitchen was transformed. Stacks of large, clear plastic boxes with lids stood three high, bearing labels such as 'books', 'main raffle' and 'tombola' while her table was a mass of coloured material triangles which she had begun to sew onto one long string.

"I'm helping Beth," said Rachel, smiling, "We're raising money for equipment for the baby unit."

"Why?" he growled.

"Because the hospital needs another special incubator. When Ffion went in to have her baby..."

"I meant, what's in it for you?"

Rachel stared at Oliver's red face. "What do you mean?"

"Are you pregnant?" He looked at her flat stomach and tiny waist.

The Standing Stone – The Gathering

"No I am not! Not that it's any of your business! Look, you give to cancer research charities even if you don't have cancer!"

"I don't!"

"Fine, well I do! Anyway, what's it to you if I want to help Beth? I've enjoyed this past week thank you, until you came along!"

"She's trying to keep us apart," said Oliver, sitting at the table and running his hand through his hair. Hazel eyes looked at Rachel from beneath his soft fringe. "I'm sorry, I overreacted."

"What's this all about?"

Oliver looked at his watch. "We'll miss the film at Cellan."

"Sod the film!" said Rachel, sitting in the chair at her sewing machine, "I want to know what's eating you!"

An hour later, Rachel opened a second bottle of red wine and giggled at Oliver sitting upright on the sofa with a large fluffy black and white cat in his lap.

"He likes you." She bit her lip but another giggled escaped.

"I can't move," whispered Oliver, "Every time I move he digs his claws in."

Rachel curled into a ball on the floor and laughed. "You look so funny!"

"Glad I amuse you."

"Oh, lighten up," said Rachel, wiping tears from her eyes. "I'll feed him."

Rachel returned from the kitchen to find Oliver in front of the fire, picking cat hair from his sweater.

"Leave it," she said, "Have another glass of wine." She sat on the sofa with the bottle and patted the seat next to her.

"It's ruined."

"It's just a sweater."

Oliver spun round and faced her. "A very expensive sweater."

"I'll buy you another."

"What?"

"If my cat has ruined your terribly important sweater, I'll buy you another," said Rachel, taking a swig from the bottle, "In fact, I'll buy you two. Happy now?"

Oliver sat beside her, taking the bottle and filling their glasses. "I'm not used to animals."

"I know. Beth told me about the dog using your sweater for bedding," said Rachel, grinning, "You're not having a lot of luck with sweaters, are you?" She lay her head on his shoulder.

"You're laughing at me."

"Not at you, with you and why shouldn't I laugh?" said Rachel, sitting up and draining her glass, "I've not had much to laugh about since Christmas."

"Point taken, sorry."

"And that's why I offered to help Beth. It'll be fun."

"If you think so," said Oliver, refilling her glass, "I don't want it to take all your time though."

"Why?"

"You know I like spending time with you."

Rachel blushed and took a gulp of her wine. Oliver put his arm round her shoulders and drew her to him.

"I needed something to do," said Rachel, "And I wanted to be useful and appreciated. Having oodles of money is all very well but I'm too young to be a lady of leisure."

"You could travel. There's a whole world out there."

Rachel shook her head. "This is my home. I feel safe here."

"It's very quiet."

"You regretting your move?"

"A little, I guess. There has to be a balance. I didn't ever seem to get away from work, living in London and now, I'm constantly looking for excitement."

"Oh, right," said Rachel, sitting up and punching his arm, "You want me to be your excitement in Wales."

With smooth swift movements, Oliver put their wine glasses on the coffee table, wrapped his arms around her and kissed her. She began to push him away but he held her tighter, his lips caressing hers with gentle, succulent kisses that travelled to her neck and back to her lips. She relaxed into his arms and began to kiss him back until, she opened her eyes and realised what she was doing. She pushed him away and as his hold tightened, gave him a shove.

Oliver sat back. "What's the matter?"

Rachel shook her head. "Too soon."

Oliver stroked her cheek and smiled. "I thought you were having fun. Isn't that what you want?"

He handed her the wine glass but she put it back on the table, shaking her head again. "Too many consequences and it's too soon for...well..."

"We're friends," said Oliver, "and you are beautiful so I kissed you. Here, I'll lay my cards on the table if it helps. I'm new here and so are you. I like spending time with you. I want to explore Wales and I'd like to do it with you. I'm self employed so work is flexible."

Rachel watched him, her fingers itching for another feel of his muscled chest. She liked the idea he presented, of a companion to share her life with.

"I thought you wanted more."

"What hot blooded male wouldn't? Don't you like me?"

"You know I do."

"Then don't make a problem where there isn't one. We can take things as slow as you like."

"But you want us to be a couple?"

"Of course! I don't want some local farmer snapping you up!"

"Can I think about it?"

"Sure, while you find me some bedding for the sofa."

"You're staying?" She stood up, her hands clenching and unclenching at her sides.

"You opened the wine!"

Oliver was gone when she stumbled downstairs at 8.30am the next morning. The note he left, scribbled on an old envelope made her heart beat faster, but whether from excited pleasure or fear, she could not tell.

'Don't think for too long. I've tickets for a show on Saturday in Cardiff. Oliver x'

The Standing Stone – The Gathering

Rachel resumed sewing her bunting at the kitchen table, singing along to 'golden oldies' on the radio. She was flattered by Oliver's attention and allowed herself to daydream about them being a couple, imagining them living in his beautiful house, hosting parties and taking weekend breaks on the Continent. He could fill the gap Marcus left in her life and she would never be lonely again. They could buy a new house together or start a new business or travel the world or all three but she knew these were dreams, pictures of how she wanted life to be as Oliver's lack of affinity with animals was already flashing warning signals in her brain.

A knock stirred her from her musings and she glanced at the kitchen clock, surprised it was early afternoon, as she went to open the door.

Beth was impressed by her plastic boxes and bunting and they discussed new stalls and ideas for the fund raiser before she started a conversation about Oliver.

"He said he stayed here last night."

"Yeah, on the sofa. We drank too much wine so he stayed."

Beth frowned and looked hard into Rachel's eyes. "Did he tell you why he left London?"

"Of course! He wants more balance in his life. Beth, what's wrong? He said you were trying to keep us apart, that you had made me help you with the fund raiser."

"Typical." Beth ran her fingers through bobbed blond curls.

"What is?"

"It's partly the truth, I suppose but the main reason he left London was that he was arrested for assault."

"Oh."

"He became obsessed with this woman he was seeing, wanting to be with her all the time and knowing what she was doing. She broke off the relationship and he followed her one night to a man's house and kicked the shit out of him. It was her brother."

"Why didn't you tell me?"

"We talked and he promised you were just friends."

"We are just friends!"

Beth raised her eyebrows.

"Okay, he kissed me last night but I stopped him. He said he wanted more but would be happy with friends and... I believed him!"

"He's a loveable man, he really is or I would have warned you off straight away but he's obsessive about stuff."

"His clothes..."

"His appearance, house, car, everything! He's only happy in a perfect world."

"I was dumb to be flattered by his persistence to see me."

"He said you called him first."

"I did but...I've given the wrong signals, haven't I?"

"Maybe but don't be hard on yourself. I've no doubt he likes you."

"But do I really want to go out with an obsessive man who worries about cat hair on his sweater?"

"Do you want to go out with anyone right now?"

Her torch lit the way as she climbed towards the mound wearing a coat over her pyjamas. Work in the garden helped her sleep but worrying about Oliver had left her restless. The hoot of an owl close to her bedroom window had kindled a desire to get outside and visit the stone circle. The moon was almost full, casting shadows at her feet as she climbed upwards. Shivering as the chill penetrated her Wellington boots, Rachel shut her eyes and laid both hands and her forehead on the standing stone. Rachel's world turned white.

Candy struggled to fall asleep in her straw bed with the sound of Aaron's breathing so close to her. They had talked into the night, Aaron trying to persuade her to go back to the village, assuring her a role could be found for her while she tried to persuade him to stay. She wasn't sure why. Maybe a solitary life wasn't what she wanted. She missed Artie and Ben despite their betrayal. Or maybe it was Binah's words, that it was Aaron's force to her form that she needed, to succeed with her plans in the Badland.

She rose early, breaking her fast alone before tending to her seeds and walking down to the river.

Aaron joined her on the riverbank. "I'll come with you to seek out your neighbours."

They planned to travel for two days and then return so the plants and sheep would need to be safe for four. They potted up seedlings and sat the new pots in a shallow trough they filled with water. Established plants received their water by drip feed from old plastic bottles, inverted in a wire holder with a twist of cable in the neck, only allowing a few drops through at a time. Once all the water troughs were full, Candy and Aaron packed their rations, including a biscuit which Candy had created using a flat metal tray over the camp fire.

The following morning they set off for the hills before the sun shone into the valley. Leaving the sheep pasture behind, they climbed the first hill, the wet grass soaking their feet. There was no proper path, merely tracks trodden by animals that afforded a little respite from wading through waist high grass and ferns. As they climbed, grass was superseded by rock and Candy stumbled often despite her staff. Into the top, in the niche where it forked, she had bound a milky white rock she found by the river which sparkled as the sun rose above them.

On the summit of the hill, with the sun nearing its zenith, they stood and surveyed the land beneath them. Behind, in the distance, they saw Candy's cottage and barns and beyond, the river winding and twisting between the trees. In front of them a patchwork of fields and valleys spread out, backed by more hills. They ate from their packs and sipped sweet river water as they scoured the landscape for signs of life.

"There!" cried Candy, standing up, her long auburn hair, no longer matted, winding and curling in the breeze.

Aaron's eyes followed to where she pointed until he too stood up, watching the tiny white dots on the hillside.

"I can't see a house."

"Neither can I," admitted Candy, "but I've counted thirty sheep up there and I'm sure I can see lambs."

"Then we should keep moving if we want to be on that hill by nightfall tomorrow."

"I'm glad you're here," said Candy, as they took sips from their water bottles before descending the hill.

"I'm still not sure I should be. I was sent to bring you back, after all."

"So why are you here then?"

"You," said Aaron, "I've never met anyone like you before."

"Well, you wouldn't. You've only spent time in the Dome with other alphas or with lesser humans, begging for their lives in the interrogation rooms."

Aaron nodded. "Maybe but you are an unusual product of the system."

"I'm not a product! I'm a person! You make me sound like a machine made in a factory!"

"How do you know about factories?"

"The Screen had archive photos. Hundreds of people, each adding to a machine until it leaves the factory as a whole product."

"You're not a machine."

"I know! Machines don't feel. They don't empathise or draw inspiration from their environment or other people. I am of this Land."

"So you do need other people?"

"If they're like minded, of course but not if all they want is to impose their rules and take away my freedom."

"What if we find people and they are not to your liking?"

"You're making fun of me."

"No, I'm thinking out loud. What if another group have established villages out here and they have rules, like the Partnering?"

"And now you're trying to scare me. I don't know what I will find but I do know I have to look."

"Because the goddess told you."

"Yes, do you have a problem with that?"

"No, just no understanding. I know nothing of gods and goddesses except some old stories I read on the Screen about what humans believed thousands of years ago."

"Anna believed me."

"She believed you had dreamed or had visions, not uncommon for those suffering from shock or deprivation."

"She was happy enough to take my plants!"

Aaron laughed, his blue eyes twinkling as they sat on a boulder half way down the hill.

"Plants can be analysed for their health properties and yours may give us an incite into the cure for the airborne sickness."

"Do you know where the sickness came from?"

Aaron shook his head. "No one does."

The Standing Stone – The Gathering

Candy remembered the images she was shown by the goddess of the moon. She saw the huge explosion, the mushroom cloud and the screams of the people as their bodies were burned and maimed. She said nothing.

They descended the third hill that day as the sun sank in the sky and the cool damp evening fell upon them. They made for the shores of a lake, eager to see if there was life there but as they neared the waters edge, with candle lit lanterns from the cottage to guide them, the outline of a single standing stone came into view.

Candy ran to the stone. She put down her lantern and still clasping her staff, used her other hand to grasp the standing stone. Candy's world turned white.

Denying what she had seen with her eyes was a futile task but Fern tried it anyway, desperate to alleviate the pain which constricted her heart. Never before had she doubted Adalwin's love and the surety she felt that they would always be together but the way he had looked into Mara's eyes had betrayed him and his father's happiness and wishes would not be denied. Stumbling to the mound, she cried hot tears for a future stripped from her by the three people she most loved and respected next to Nia and Rowan. She wept for the future she had imagined for herself. Would she become like Nia, bereft of the man she loved, only serving the villagers, guiding them through their lives?

She climbed the final steep paces onto the mound and ran sobbing to the Standing Stone. Fern grasped the stone and her world turned white.

A gleaming silver world lay before the women as they sat on the lime green grass. From behind the Standing Stone the outline of a woman emerged. As one, the women stood, smiling at each other, recognition evident in their eyes as they turned to face the goddess.

Long, dark auburn hair hung to her waist, flicking around her as a soft breeze rose up. She wore a simple natural cotton shift, tied with a plaited cord while all around her danced tiny stars like motes of dust, charged with unseen energy. Vivid green eyes shone in the elfin face of the goddess, Rhiannon.

Fern stepped forward, boldly holding out her arms, tears streaming from her eyes as she stood in the golden glow of the goddess.

"I know your pain," whispered Rhiannon, her green eyes full of kindness, "You feel you are losing him."

"He is lost," sobbed Fern, bowing her head.

"You must not give up. All that I loved was taken from me but I never lost hope."

"But how can I stand by and watch? How can I watch the man I love be taken by another?"

"Never stop loving him, child, never. Do not fight with anger and bitterness but with love and commitment to your duty."

"I know my duty."

"Then be strong. Fill your heart and mind with love. Carry it always. Love never dies."

"But what is love?" said Rachel, stepping forward, "I believed my husband loved me but since his death, all I've felt is the pain of his betrayal and lies."

"He loved you, child, of this you must not doubt so why do you seek another?"

"I didn't seek him!"

"Didn't you? Did you not see in this new man the hopes you had for the first?"

Rachel hung her head.

"Your reaction is predictable, no one blames you but stop seeking elsewhere for the love you need."

"So I'm to die alone and unloved?"

"You know the answer, Rachel. Trust yourself. Trust the Land."

"That's what I'm doing," said Candy, taking Rachel's hand and squeezing it. "In my life, so different and distant from yours, I'm relying on myself and the Land."

"And the Whisperer?" said Rhiannon.

"He wants me to go with him, back to the villages."

"Yet you've asked him to stay with you."

"I want him to stay. I like him. I..want to know him better."

"And yet you want to believe you can help the people of the earth by following him?"

"I don't know! He says the scientists can find a cure for the sickness and I can help them."

"Trust yourself, Candy. Your staff will guide you. Remain steadfast in your resolve."

"And me?" asked Fern.

"Be a warrior with the heart of a goddess, Fern and Rachel, embrace the spirit of the horse."

A breeze picked up, fluttering their hair as the brilliance blew around them, filling their limbs with energy and their hearts with the freedom of the hills. Their noses twitched to the scents of the Land; grass after a sudden cloudburst and the earth as the snow melts away. They heard the wind blowing through the leafy boughs and its roars, echoing around snowy mountain peaks. With their faces glowing and their eyes bright with hope, they placed one hand upon the Standing Stone.

Chapter 4

Rachel piled dry kindling onto the embers in the burner and left them to ignite while she went to find her lantern. With hot chocolate beside her and the burner piled with logs, she lit her candle and sat looking into the flame. Merlin joined her, curling into her lap while Angel Face sat in front of the burner. Night descended on the lounge but rather than depositing its usual burden of loneliness, Rachel's lantern illuminated the darkness, filling her heart with the beauty of the Land.

The following morning, Rachel made her call. "Hi, Oliver, it's me."

"Rachel, I'm glad you called."

"We need to talk."

"I know. Beth told me she spoke to you."

"You lied to me."

"What I said was true and I meant it but I just..."

"Didn't tell me everything."

Silence.

"Are you free during the day tomorrow?" asked Rachel.

"I've appointments in the morning but I can cancel them."

"No, don't do that. It's going to be a fine afternoon so I thought we could have a picnic."

"Okay, where do you want to go?"

"I'd like to stay here. Let's have a picnic on my Land."

"What about the show in Cardiff?"

Silence.

"Rachel?"

The words she spoke now would decide her future. She felt safe in the silence, alone in her head full of dreams and possible futures yet she needed to speak. "We need to talk."

Candy picked up the lantern at her feet and turned to find Aaron sat on a rock by the lake. He came towards her, his face shiny wet with tears.

"You came back," he said, grasping her shoulder and pulling her to him. "I thought I'd lost you."

"Of course I came back."

"Where did you go? You were shimmering like a star, whispering words and talking to the air and then...I couldn't see you at all."

"I was with Rachel and Fern and the goddess Rhiannon."

"I don't understand. I mean, how could you..."

Candy pulled back from him. She was growing accustomed to his face and though dirty and tear stained, she resisted the urge to kiss it. Confusion, doubt and fear radiated from him and she wanted to reassure him.

"I found a standing stone down the tunnel by my guard post Below in the Dome. I thought it was the only one but you saw the one by the pool when Anna saved you and now, this one by the lake. The stones are linked somehow. They take me to another place."

"But how do Rachel and Fern get there?"

"I don't know."

"What did the goddess tell you?"

Candy shook her head. "We need to find shelter. The wind's picking up. Come on."

Early the following morning, Sky and River joined Fern for their first hunting trip. Fern's face grew hot as Adalwin and two Tall Folk joined them at Adalbern's long house. Adalwin issued instructions to stay close together before they set off into the forest.

They made good speed for a while until the trees grew more dense and Adalwin and the men began to point out signs of animal activity to the novices. Gnawed stems, animal droppings and footprints were scrutinized and discussed until Fern wondered whether they would ever begin hunting and then she caught a scent she didn't recognise and stood up.

Adalwin reached to pull her down but their eyes met and both turned their heads to the wind.

Sky and River chatted and laughed as they followed the carcass of the boar but Fern walked beside Adalwin in silence as they dragged the meat to the village. The Gathering, with its opportunity for trade, could not come quickly enough if they were going to preserve similar food for the winter. Maybe they should acquire even more salt then they planned, especially if the river continued its abundance of fish. While Fern's head organised her village duties, her heart cried out to the man beside her.

They stopped and took a drink from the water skin and Fern felt his gaze warm her face. She turned with a smile which Adalwin met with one of his own.

The abundance of spring moved towards summer in the village and the three tribes worked together as, each day, the sun rose warmer and stayed longer. Plants, animals and women brought forth new life.

The morning of the full moon was a hot cloudless one and the villagers were caught up in the excitement of the evening ritual to come. Food was prepared and wood stacked ready for the ritual fire, a separate one from the cooking fire. This was a ceremony of fire and light and they intended to show the gods how dedicated they were in their worship.

Fern helped with the food, new lambs and new babies before sitting on her sleeping mat and weaving a garland of her own. Her dark hair reached to her waist and she twisted it together and wore it down the side of her face. Unlike Mara's matted tresses, Fern teased hers out with a bone comb and this evening, she planned to wear it loose. With her willow headdress complete, save for a few more flowers, she heard her name and rose to greet the enquirer.

Adalwin pulled back the skin over the doorway and stepped into the house. Though shadows filled the interior, she saw sadness in his eyes. Without explanation, he pulled her to him and kissed her. Every second of his kiss lasted a minute and every minute, an hour. Enveloped in his embrace, feeling his lips, the roughness of his chin, Fern recognised the love she felt.

There was lust, of course, desire and longing to be entwined with his naked body forever but this love was so much more.

When he parted from her, she touched his face and saw the sadness return to his eyes.

Chapter 5

They walked the pathway she'd mown through the grass until they reached the circle beneath the apple trees. Though gnarly and mossy in parts, new branches, new leaves and sweet apple blossom effused from the trees. It was a perfect spot for a picnic.

Oliver hated the blanket, the flies, the ants and even the breeze, as it blew stray grass onto his food. Rachel had made egg mayonnaise and cress sandwiches, which were too salty and the crusts too hard, and an apple cake which was too tart.

In less than an hour, Rachel reached her decision. She lay back on the blanket, her hair splaying out onto the grass behind her. Blue sky peeped out from beneath the foliage and the odd wispy white cloud drifted across her vision.

"It's such a beautiful day. Lie down and look at the sky."

"You're all right."

Rachel rolled onto her stomach. "It won't work, Oliver. We're too different."

"Of course we're not. You said yourself, we can do anything, go anywhere."

"But what if all I want is to stay here, lie on the grass and watch the clouds go by?"

"You don't."

"You mean, you don't! I'm sorry. You don't seem happy here in Wales."

"It's all the mess and confusion with moving but it won't be for much longer. I'll have my own house soon."

"And then what?"

"I'll be happier...we'll be happier."

Rachel shook her head.

Oliver sat with his arms around his knees. "I thought you wanted more from life than just this." He gestured at the trees and the land beyond. "You're far too good for this."

"You mean me on my digger in my overalls and Wellington boots?"

"You're not that person, Rachel. I want to dress you in silk and diamonds and have you on my arm at film premières and smart restaurants."

"Why would I want to do that?"

"To be seen. You deserve to be in the best company."

"By best you mean richest?"

"You said you had money."

"What if I didn't? What if I hadn't a penny?"

Oliver frowned before stopping abruptly, pressing the worry lines on his forehead flat with his fingers as he spoke. "But you have."

"I shouldn't have told you. You needed to know me without that."

"Know you?" Oliver stood up. "You don't even know yourself! Beth has obviously brainwashed you into believing I'm some sort of control freak and you're a...a...bloody hippy like her!"

Rachel stifled the laughter bubbling inside her but couldn't help a smile. "Sit down. No one's brainwashing me, I assure you. My decisions are my own."

A warm glow spread to her face as she spoke and a lightness filled her heart and limbs. "You're right, I don't know myself as well as I should and I'm taking the time to do that but I rejected a drink and a date when we first met, do you remember? That was my gut instinct and it was correct. I'm not ready to start dating."

They sat, sipping beer as the swallows chattered and giggled above them and the bees hummed among the blossom.

"So where does that leave us?"

"There is no 'us', Oliver."

"So I can't see you?"

"Let's leave it a while, don't you think? Maybe we can be mates in the future, when you get sorted."

"There's nothing wrong with me, I assure you," said Oliver, flicking a fly off his jeans. "I made a mistake with Martha and I've learned from that. End of."

"I mean sorted in your house and work, so you're less stressed."

"Forget it, Rachel. I know when I'm dumped." He stood up.

"It's not..." said Rachel, standing next to him.

"Please, spare me the excuses. Have a nice life."

Oliver turned and walked away.

"Wait, what about..."

She stood shaking her head as Oliver strode off to his car. Sadness washed over her and she sat down on the

The Standing Stone – The Gathering

blanket, surveying the picnic remains which she would need to transport back to the house. Once she wiped away her tears, a feeling of peace swept over her shoulders as she gathered the blanket and walked towards the back door. She had worried that saying goodbye to Oliver would be losing a friend from her life but she could see now that he was far too self absorbed to be the kind of friend she wanted. As she returned for a second trip to the orchard, a sense of freedom fell over her and excitement quivered through her blood.

She could go off travelling or jet off for a weekend in the sun but she was free to choose and right now, she needed to be home in Wales.

Candy and Aaron set off early the following morning, eating biscuits as they walked. Sleep had been fitful and disturbed for Candy, she presumed after her encounter with the goddess and she tried to dismiss the feelings of unease from her mind. The valley opened out before them, sheep grazing on both steep sides and ahead, beyond a bend in the river, smoke rose to greet them.

She quickened her pace, excited to meet those who she was sure were her nearest neighbours when a shot rang out, followed by another. Aaron pushed her to the ground and pulled a hand gun from his pack, crouching and looking for any signs of movement.

"Put it away!" cried Candy, "Why have you brought a gun?"

"You have one," said Aaron, scanning the landscape.

"Not here, not to meet other survivors!" She sat up. "Put it away!"

Aaron turned to her, his eyes full of fear. "This place isn't called the Badland for nothing."

A shout ahead of them, followed by two more brought a group of people into their eye line. Aaron aimed his hand gun.

"No!" Candy pushed him to the ground and sat on him, fighting to take the gun. "These are my people! Put the gun away!"

With the gun out of sight and their backpacks on, they walked slowly towards the people with their hands up.

"Stop!"

They stopped.

"Are you sick?"

"No!" cried Candy. "We come from over there!" She gestured behind her.

"Keep walking slowly!"

They met in the middle of the valley, beside the banks of a river bedecked with trees brimming with white blossom and Candy wept at the sight of four men, four women and two small children who stood before them. One man held a rifle pointing at them but a young woman pushed forward and took Candy into her arms. They clung to each other until the man lowered his rifle and they were beckoned to follow.

With a cup of grassy smelling tea in her hand, Candy told the story of her ejection from the Dome and setting up home in the little cottage after running away from the village of Three Oaks. She ate a warm filling milky

The Standing Stone – The Gathering

porridge while Aaron explained that he had come to find her. The surprise on the faces of their hosts confirmed that they knew nothing of the Dome, until Katya, the young woman who had embraced Candy, spoke.

"Before Grandpa died, his mind was confused. He talked about a religious cult. They were to build an ark to protect them from a terrible disaster soon to befall the earth."

"What sort of disaster?" asked Candy.

"He didn't say, just that the earth would be devastated and only they would survive."

"Could anyone join them?"

Katya shook her head. "They were the Chosen Ones. Then the earth shook, the satellites in the sky fell to earth and flames devoured the land and life upon it."

"When did this happen?"

"Grandpa's been gone ten years, he was sixty something...it must be forty years ago."

Candy looked around at the people in the farmhouse kitchen. Some sat on chairs, others on the floor in front of the fire. None of them was over forty years of age.

"So you were born here?"

"Yes," said Katya, "There are four more families, further up the valley who we work with, help each other out but we've never seen anyone from your direction."

Candy wept inside for the old couple in her cottage who had lived and died alone with neighbours so close by. But they had managed and survived and lived a free life, unlike the poor souls in the Dome. How could the world have been decimated in only forty years? Where did this notion of a religious cult come from? She had been taught that the Dome had been erected to save All from the sickness brought about by the Great Maker but she had queried that fact for a long while so who had set off such a devastating explosion and why?

"So beyond your neighbours, is there sickness in the air?" asked Aaron.

Katya shook her head.

"So how do you know about it?"

"We travel to the Trading twice a year. After harvest and for the longest day of the year. Travellers come from all over and news of the sickness reached us there. No one knows how far it spreads or whether countries, or even continents, have living people left on them."

"What do you call this place?" asked Candy.

"Come and see," said Katya, taking her hand.

While Aaron stayed behind, conversing with two of the men, the rest of the people followed Candy and Katya out to the back of the farm. Cows mingled in the fields with the sheep as they walked up the hill, into the shade where a chill wind blew. Katya pointed to the fields on the other side of the river. Horses grazed, brown, chestnut and black, and new foals rolled in the grass beside their mothers.

"They come from all over this land," said Katya, "Wild on the hillside but docile to the touch. This is Dyffryn y Ceffyl, Valley of the Horse."

The villagers kept the ritual fire burning into the night, drumming and dancing by the light of its flame. As the children and Olds were bedded down, men and women took to their feet and celebrated the life giving fire with their dance. Couples began to break away, disappearing into the darkness. Fern danced with Sky and River.

Mara had danced with them at first, naked except for a leather skirt beneath her cape but she danced by the men now, delighting at their faces as they stared at her painted body and naked breasts. Even knowing how she felt about Adalwin, Fern liked Mara, her forthright words and sensible, practical thinking but she disliked the way she taunted the men with her body, daring them to touch her.

Adalwin sat beside his father Adalbern, watching Mara, fixated by the gyrating, curvaceous woman dancing to the beat. She turned and danced facing the men and Adalwin rose and walked towards her, stopping on the edge of the circle of fire.

Fern stopped too, holding her breath as the drum beat changed. Instead of the pounding, mesmerizing beat, a new rhythm struck up and all the dancers fell away except Fern, Mara and Adalwin. Mara continued her dance, her hips circling, her legs splayed and her arms spread wide, leaving space for her ample breasts to jiggle and bounce in front of Adalwin. Fern circled around the fire to the tempo and stillness within the new beat. Unaware of anything but the fire and the drum, her body moved to the music of the earth and knew how to encapsulate its gentleness as well as its power. Twisting, turning and spinning, her feet kept their balance while her hips and shoulders picked out the accents of the drum beats, rising to a crescendo of shimmies before falling again to the lilting song of a gentle stream.

On she danced, her eyes only for the fire, taking into her body the power and beauty of the flames as she circled her wrists and spun on her toes until the rhythm dwindled and only a single drum beat remained. Then she saw him watching her. Adalwin, her Adalwin. His eyes were no longer sad but full of longing for her, as he took her hand and led her into the forest.

Chapter 6

She rang Beth and told her the outcome of the conversation with Oliver at the picnic, before stoking up the burner and taking a bath. Sitting in the tub up to her chin in bubbles, Rachel analysed how she felt about being alone. Every waking morning was a lottery. Some days, the little stone house felt like home as she welcomed the cats with their breakfast while on others, she dragged her limbs from her safe, warm cave and faced the world with trepidation.

Rhiannon was correct, of course. Oliver had seemed the perfect solution to the hurt and pain of her life; a handsome, kind man and a perfect home, a love to last forever in idyllic happiness. She had thought that was the life she wanted but Oliver's perfection was itself a disorder, not a solution and a life full of money bought pleasures was a shallow existence, not a rich, fulfilling experience. It seemed she was getting to know herself and though she did not yet know what she wanted to do with her life, she was beginning to understand what made her happy.

She wiped her mirror with the edge of a towel and stood it on the side of the bath. Sad eyes looked back at her and she peered forward to examine her skin more closely around them, pulling at the corners. Instead of laughter lines, downward drooping crows feet were forming. She threw herself back, water slushing out of the tub.

The ache in her heart poked at her pride, confirming what she already knew. She missed Rhys, his laughter and his smile. He'd been so kind and she'd thrown away a genuine friendship.

The following morning, the post arrived early, including a letter from Lucy Pinder. Rachel took it into the garden to read with her coffee and toast. While the finches chattered around her, Rachel learned that Lucy was coming to Wales at the end of June and wanted to meet up or, if possible, stay for a few days.

She digested the missive, thinking back to the teenage years they had spent together. Horses had been the prominent feature in Lucy's life and she had looked after and ridden her own pony from the age of five. An elegant, rambling Georgian house came into Rachel's mind and the warm, musky smells of the stables, where she had helped Lucy with her pony. Memories of sweet straw tickling her nose, her warm breath rising as they helped groom the other horses and giggles about boys, warmed Rachel's heart. Rhiannon's words 'Embrace the spirit of the horse' shone in the forefront of her mind.

She ran indoors to fetch the cordless phone and called Lucy before pulling on her beanie hat and heading for her raised beds. Tiny weeds had already started to form, which she removed into her barrow before unpacking her nursery delivery.

Her book had described the Three Sisters method of planting sweetcorn, beans and squashes so, as the plot she had chosen was a little breezy, this seemed an ideal plan to begin her vegetable garden. She loved the idea

The Standing Stone – The Gathering

that the 'sisters' helped each other, the sweetcorn supporting the beans while they in turn, stabilized the corn from toppling in the wind and the squashes smothered the emerging weeds and prevented water evaporating from the soil.

Although she was a novice to vegetable growing, with her tattered book to guide her, Rachel felt a sense of purpose rising through her. She abandoned her gloves, preferring to handle the plants and earth with her hands. She ignored her stained and chipped nails, delving deep into the soil and wishing her vegetables well in their new fertile home.

She was so engrossed with her planting that she failed to hear a car pull onto the drive, only aware she had a visitor when she heard her name called.

"Over here!" she called back.

Rhys walked towards her, making her heart thump as she dropped her trowel in the earth and ran towards him. She surprised herself by throwing herself into his arms.

"Thank you for that lovely, if unexpected welcome," said Rhys, hugging her back.

"I missed you and I'm so sorry," she said, burying her face into his thick, hemp t-shirt. "I've been such a fool."

"I've been worried about you but there's no need to apologise."

"But there is!"

Rachel ground fresh coffee beans and they sat in the back garden. "So much has happened in just one month."

"Tell me," said Rhys.

She told him everything from her weakness with Oliver to the Midsummer fund raiser for the baby unit and Lucy's impending visit, a little ashamed but determined to be honest.

"Sounds like you're finding yourself again."

"Not again. I've never stood up and said 'This is me' before. I've always been a 'me' for others and looked to everyone else for the love I craved."

"And now?"

Rachel sat back, nursing her mug in her lap, afraid to meet Rhys' eyes.

"The Goddess Rhiannon spelt it out for me. She knew, you see, she knew I thought Oliver was the answer but I'll never find love from a partner, if that's what I want, until I learn to love myself."

"How does that realisation feel?"

"Scary but exciting. I feel like I'm taking responsibility for my own life and living the way I believe. Standing up to Oliver was the first step and being involved with Beth's project is another."

"Has Ishtar's lantern helped?"

Rachel shook her head. "I light it, look into the flame and feel her connection but I don't feel she's guiding me or anything."

"Give it time, keep trusting and maybe you need less help than you thought you did. How are the veg beds coming on?"

"I'd neglected them until this morning. Come and see."

The Standing Stone – The Gathering

"It's amazing what a new moon can do," said Rhys, rising to join her.

They stayed the night with Katya and her partner, Grant, helping with the animals to earn their supper. Candy wished she could stay longer and learn more about growing food and looking after animals.

The following morning, Candy gratefully accepted the provisions Katya gave her and filled her backpack.

"You must come back before the longest day," said Katya, "We can travel together to the Trading."

"I don't know. It will mean leaving my cottage for many days."

"Well, the offer's there and you are both welcome."

"Aaron may not stay, you see. He only ventured to the Badland to look for me."

Katya laughed. "Is that really what you call it? You'll have to find a different name for your home!"

"I know, there's nothing bad here."

"And Aaron wants to stay with you but something, or someone, has a strong hold on his actions."

"You can feel that?"

Katya nodded.

"All I feel is that he's not telling me everything, that he's keeping an important truth from me. Oh, I don't know!"

"You do know, be patient," said Katya, taking her hand. "Come, I have a gift for you."

Around the back of the farmhouse, tied with a soft rope as a halter stood a brown horse with a black mane and tail.

"This is Afon," said Katya, stroking the horse's neck, "It means 'river'"

"He's beautiful," said Candy, stroking the horse. She laughed as he nuzzled her, rubbing his soft, downy nose on her neck.

"He's yours," said Katya.

"Oh, I couldn't! How could I repay you? I've nothing to trade for a horse."

"His mother is a favourite of mine called Ella. She's a wonderful mother, so tender and gentle yet she's strong and brave. Her son is the same. Take him and you can get back to us sooner."

"Really?"

"Yes!" laughed Katya, hugging her. "I've not made a new friend...well, ever! Please promise that you will come back for the Trading now?"

Candy laughed too making Afon back away from them. "Okay, I'll be here by the second new moon."

They walked along the valley floor, Candy wiping away stray tears, leading Afon on a long rein while Aaron walked ahead, seeming in a hurry to get back to the cottage.

That night they ate early from the pack Katya had given them before Candy rubbed Afon down with the brush Katya had provided and Aaron went into the wood, in search of privacy. Only when the light began to fail and he did not return did Candy realise he had taken his pack with him. She chose the path he had taken and inched her way into the darkness of the close growing trees. After a few moments she heard him talking and the strange echoing response of another voice. She moved closer to hear the conversation.

"...home by tomorrow night but it isn't going to be easy to persuade her."

"Keep her at the cottage then and I will send a team to pick you both up."

"No, father, no! Let me try. If she comes with me freely, she will take to her new home more easily."

"As you wish but I'm not giving you much longer. If you can't persuade her, leave your comm in the cottage emitting the emergency signal and we'll get a fix on you. It shouldn't take more than a week to get to you."

"I'm sure I can manage."

"See you do. We need her here. She may have wild ways that need to be tamed but her intelligence and obvious psychic abilities are valuable to us. We need to know more about the power of these stones. Don't disappoint me."

"I won't, father."

As the conversation ended, Candy crept back to their camp site. With a blanket round her shoulders, she curled into the roots of a tree completely encased in ivy and though she pretended sleep for a few moments while her heartbeat dropped back to normal, within minutes she was dreaming. She lay beneath the tree, looking up at the night sky. No longer was each twinkle of light a single star, but she saw the network, like an astral cobweb, that bound them all together. She too became caught up in the web, bound to Aaron but also his father. Another thread linked her to Katya and this blossomed outward, like ripples in a pond, tiny points of light in the waves, the people she had yet to meet.

While the men continued building the boats, the women and children worked on the weaving house, which was to be the Boat People's home for the winter months. Fine weather gave them long hours of sunshine in which to work and when tired of the physical labour of covering the lattice panels in their muddy coating, they sat in the shade making mittens or plaiting reed for baskets to sell at the Gathering. By the end of a hot week, the first boat was finished and the whole village, helping the Olds, went down to the water's edge to see her take to the water.

Though the main body of the boat was just a hollowed out log, the design sat well balanced in the water and soon the children were squealing for a ride across the river. Food and drink were brought out and one of the Boat People played a reed pipe so work was abandoned for the day in favour of a celebration picnic with songs and dancing. To one song, they accompanied with clapping and the children danced in a ring, first turning it one way and then the other.

Fern sat on the bank, leaning back into Adalwin, happy with his arms around her. They watched the dancing and joined in the songs but neither felt the need to break away to dance. As the riverbank echoed with the sound of music and laughter, Mara coaxed Adalbern to his feet and soon he was skipping and laughing with Mara in his arms. Fern turned wide eyed to Adalwin and he shrugged and smiled while Fern resumed her contented watch on the happy scene, relieved that Mara had found a new admirer but a little concerned as to what this would mean to Adalwin and the village. But today was for celebration, even Nia danced with the children though she declined a ride in the boat.

"I'm a child of the Land," she told Fern, as she sat down beside her, getting her breath back from her exertion, "I keep my feet firmly on it, where they belong."

Fern accepted Adalwin's hand to take her to the river and they walked downstream, wobbling on the slippery rocks, disturbing a water vole and a dipper as they went. As the sounds of music and laughter quietened behind them, Adalwin pulled her to a small stony inlet and kissed her. They scrambled up the bank and walked deeper into the forest before Adalwin laid down his cloak beneath an oak tree and made love to her. They lay wrapped together, Adalwin practising the words and phrases he had learned from Geirr and Fern learning their meaning in Adalwin's language. Thirsty, they started back towards the river, stumbling on weary legs as they descended to the water. Less than twenty paces away, Adalwin turned to Fern behind him and put his finger to his lips. There was another couple in the stony inlet.

Adalwin crept closer but Fern stayed back, wanting to give them privacy just as she and Adalwin had sought. Even from her distance away, Fern could hear the noisy couple and turned away, walking further into the trees. After some time, Adalwin joined her. His face was hot and flushed but whether from the heat of the day or the sight he had witnessed, she could not tell and she pulled him to the ground to kiss him before he could speak.

As a chill descended on the land, Fern and Adalwin made there way back up the river. There was no sign of the other love makers. The party on the river was moving back to the village with tired grizzly children and hot, cross parents. Fern carried Hugh the toddler in her arms and his sister, Luna, in a basket on her back while Adalwin carried a large basket of left over food and a crying baby in the nook of his arm.

Thoughts of warriors attacking the village left the minds of Fern's village as, after just one day of torrential rain, the sun shone daily for another week. As the lattice panels of the weaving house were almost complete, dividers were made for the inside as well as new hurdles for the prospective new sheep pens.

The river was plentiful with fish so the last of the precious salt was used to preserve them and Belle spoke to Fern about a story Ciara had told her. Ciara was an Old of great years and wisdom who had passed on much memory and learning to Nia and the other women, before she had departed to live with the ancestors.

"She talked about a smoking house," said Belle as they sat pulling reed into lengths. Their fingers and thumbs were bound with leather to stop the serrated edges cutting into their flesh.

"Smoking food?"

Belle nodded. "Fish and meat. Salting first and then smoking, makes both last much longer. With the village growing, I thought you could think on it. The weaving house only needs a roof now. A smoking house doesn't need to be big, just tall enough to hang the food above the smouldering fires."

"It's a good idea, Belle but more work for the men. I think Adalwin and Adalhard are beginning clearing more land beyond their father's long house soon."

"The smaller trees would be good for a smoking house. Fern, we women can build this."

"Do you think?"

"We need help at first, I'll grant you but we can erect a house ourselves. Aled is working with a group of men from our village, cutting and bending the coppiced wood to make hedges for new animals but they can help us get started."

"And the roof for the weaving house?"

Belle smiled. "Nia has Rowan and Bramble working on that."

"Really?"

"She promised them another ride in the boat if they helped her."

"Good for Nia," said Fern, "I can't keep Rowan's mind on anything for more than a moment! Who will mind the children if we build a smoking house?"

"The Olds are outside in this weather so they can keep an eye or rock a babe."

Fern nodded and continued her work until a reed flipped back and nicked her cheek. "Ow! Enough!" She sat back and touched her face.

"So you'll think on it?"

Fern laughed. "I already have, though we should call Council."

"Must we?"

"We should."

"Even though this will help feed the village and make produce for next year at the Gathering? We could try out different types of smoke too. Different tree dust makes different smoke."

"I will speak to Nia tonight. She will know what is best to do."

Belle nodded. "You'll have to make the decisions one day, Fern, just as your mother did."

Fern smiled. "I know but Nia not only looked after me and Rowan but she took on my mother's role as wise woman and healer to you all. I still have much to learn."

The evening was hot and humid, clouds trapping in the warm air on the land. Once the children were settled, the villagers sat outside their huts, talking quietly and passing round a jug of beer. Fern sought out Nia who she found with the new lambs. There was just one sheep and one lamb in a pen. Nia had tied the skin of the sheep's dead lamb around the back of the lamb whose mother had delivered triplets but was struggling to feed them. With gentle soft coos and maas, she encouraged the sheep to smell the lamb. As Fern watched, the lamb began to bleat as the sheep nuzzled her and the next moment, the hungry lamb was sucking happily on a teat.

They walked into the muggy night together and made a circuit of the village, talking about the celebration on the river bank and the progress on the weaving house. They walked almost to the watch huts before Fern explained Belle's plan to Nia.

"It is a very good idea," said Nia, "but we do have to call Council. Don't worry, we'll do it early in the morning. I can't see any objections to more food for the winter though!"

As they circled back up around Adalbern's long house, Nia leaned into Fern and took her arm.

"Are you well?" asked Fern.

"Just a little weary, that's all. The heat saps the energy from my legs and I grow old."

"You're not old!"

"I have seen almost two hundred seasons, Fern. That is old!"

"And my mother..."

"Was younger than I and younger than you are now when you were born."

"I wish I remembered her, had a memory of her to hold with me."

Nia turned to Fern and stopped her as the final light fled from the sky. "If you want to see your mother. Look into the sacred pool behind the mound. Look deep into the water and you will see her."

"Thank you, I will."

Nia took Fern's arm and they continued towards their house. "And if you want to see your father..."

Fern gasped and gripped Nia's arm. "Yes?"

"Look at Rowan. She is just like him."

"Ah, I will."

Chapter 7

With Rhys' help, Rachel planted her raised vegetable bed, banging in stakes to support the sweetcorn and train the French beans. Pumpkins and a squash called 'Peter Pan' were planted beneath them.

"That little fellow will be me then. I don't intend on growing up!"

"Life has a habit of forcing adulthood on you, don't you think?"

"I live a simple life, you know that. Mr Evans lets me borrow his van or if he's using it, Huw at the farm has a beaten up Land Rover. I don't earn enough to pay tax and my national insurance is paid twice a year by the bank. I live with cash and barter mainly."

"What do you barter?"

Rhys stood up from the raised bed, rubbing his back. "I give guitar lessons to children or adults. Sometimes I'm called upon at a get together to provide some entertainment."

"Would you play for me?"

"Sure. It's Beltane eve tonight. I could come back later if you like."

"Tell me about Beltane," said Rachel, taking off her gloves.

While Rhys explained the meaning behind the fire festival, they stacked the barrow and swept the area around the raised beds.

"So it's Rhiannon's festival?"

"For me, yes. She symbolises darkness and light, death and rebirth."

"So why now?"

"In the Celtic year there are just two seasons, winter and summer and with the beginning of summer, Beltane is a new hope and new light that comes into the world. Rhiannon's son is returned to her at Beltane."

A fine grey veil of sadness fell across Rachel's face but she swallowed the lump in her throat as they stowed away the tools. She made drinks while Rhys lit the wood burner and they sat watching the bright new flames devour the kindling.

"Tell me Rhiannon's story," said Rachel.

The sun was dipping behind the hills when Rachel and Rhys set off for the mound. Rachel had cried over Rhiannon's story and in Rhys' arms she spoke, in broken words, of her baby, Jack. Rhys held her, stroking her hair, whispering words of empathy as the torrent of pain left her body. With a bowl of pasta to sustain them, they talked all afternoon, sharing sad moments and happy days alike, before deciding to make preparations for the ritual on the mound. While Rachel showered, Rhys returned home for his guitar and provisions.

Dressed alike in green shifts and grey trousers provided by Rhys, Rachel smiled as she added her contribution to the altar before the standing stone. While Rhys added candles in holders, incense and a small cauldron in the centre, Rachel placed two of her favourite photos on the altar, one of her holding Jack

The Standing Stone – The Gathering

and another of her and Lucy, smiling broadly, arms slung across the necks of two small ponies in the stable.

Once Rhys had caste the circle and called in the Elements, he suggested Rachel welcome the goddess Rhiannon.

"Oh no, I couldn't! I wouldn't know what to say!"

"Shut your eyes and call her in your mind. You'll see her and know how to address her."

"Okay."

With her eyes tight shut, Rachel thought of the green eyed goddess and in moments, she opened her eyes to see Rhiannon in front of her.

"Hello," said Rachel, "I'm learning about Beltane today from my friend Rhys and we wondered if you would like to join us?"

"It is good to see you again, Rachel. We would be honoured to join in your celebration to welcome Summer. Thank you." She rubbed the nose of a beautiful white horse, standing calmly beside her.

Rhys stood in the flickering candlelight, his face betraying the shock and delight he felt.

"Can you see her?" asked Rachel.

Rhys nodded, flicking his gaze between Rachel and the goddess.

Rachel smiled. "Shall we begin?"

Rhys lit the fire in the cauldron. "As the face of Winter turns away, we welcome Summer. We light this fire in honour of Rhiannon who protected her people and her Land without thought for herself. We feel her suffering through the winter months but today, Pryderi is returned to her and we celebrate the Sun."

"We're looking forward to the summer," said Rachel, despite her initial shyness, "We've plants in the earth, growing in the warm soil and at the end of June, I'm seeing an old school friend, Lucy, whose ponies I used to ride."

"Into the fire we burn away the pain and anguish of winter. Out of this death, new life will begin," said Rhys.

Rachel knelt on the earth to write her prayer. Though she would never forget, the injustice of Jack's death and the pain of Marcus' suicide were consumed by the fire, leaving her more able to meet the challenges ahead of her.

"I don't want to forget them," said Rachel to Rhiannon.

"They will remain in the love you have for them, rather than a heavy yoke to carry on your shoulders."

"And I'm helping fund raising for the baby unit at the hospital."

The goddess nodded. "Compassion and kindness will ease your pain."

Rhys placed his paper in the fire before bowing to Rhiannon. Sitting cross legged on the earth, he began to play. Rachel sat beside him as the gentle, sorrowful chords ascended to the sky. She clenched her knees to her body as she and the goddess listened. A second tune carried a zinging melody and a happy four count beat and without consent from her head, Rachel danced.

Around the circle she skipped and whirled, her cheeks burning and heart racing. As the tune finished, she collapsed, laughing onto the ground.

"I didn't know you could dance?"

"Neither did I!"

"I have another song," said Rhys, "I think the goddess will enjoy it."

Rhys sang Rhiannon's story, her determination to be with the man she loved, her suffering and her ultimate joy. Rachel applauded, tears in her eyes when he finished.

"I'm so sorry I laughed at you," she said, shuffling closer as he put down his guitar.

"No problem, no problem. I'm just glad you found the Land again."

They concluded the ritual, moving the cauldron to the centre of the circle and leaping over it, laughing, hand in hand. The goddess Rhiannon smiled.

Rachel said farewell to her.

"Thank you for inviting me. Those who celebrate the old ways bring magic to their lives."

In one smooth movement, Rhiannon alighted upon the bare back of the white horse and was gone.

Indoors, they drank hot chocolate around the banked up fire.

"It's been a wonderful day," said Rachel.

"One of the best," said Rhys, "Had you any idea that your connection with the goddess Rhiannon was so strong?"

"Well, no. I just shut my eyes and called her in my mind like you said. I told you I met her with Fern and Candy."

"The standing stone brings you together?"

"Yes and it doesn't have to be the same stone, Candy said. She's used three now and each has brought her to the goddess she needed."

"And brings you and Fern as well?"

"It is odd, the way our lives are linked."

"Across time and space," murmured Rhys.

Rachel lit the chunky candles in the fireplace.

"So how do you feel about life at the moment? Rhiannon has obviously inspired you."

"I'm feeling good," admitted Rachel, "Once I began to trust myself, what was important to me became clearer. I no longer feel I need someone else to make my life for me."

"Oliver?"

"Yeah, big mistake!"

"With all you've been through it's not surprising that you looked for someone to take the pain away."

"But I already had you, the best of friends but I couldn't see it."

"That's me, invisible."

"I didn't mean it like that!"

"I know, just teasing. Come here."

Rachel crawled into his arms and accepted the offered hug.

The Standing Stone – The Gathering

The final day's walk back to her cottage was a trudge through pouring rain. Once Afon had been rubbed down and made comfortable in a corner of the barn and water brought in for him, Candy and Aaron were glad of the shelter of the cottage and lit a fire in the kitchen. Candy stood lit candles on shelves and in nooks and emptied the provisions from her bag while Aaron soon produced a blaze that warmed them as they removed their wet clothing. With a towel around her, Candy found clothes for Aaron in the blanket box. They heated water first and made tea from the packet Katya had sent with them and pulled the two low rickety chairs closer to the fire. They fried bacon in a pan and ate it on a chunk of rye bread.

"It's feeling better," said Candy, wiping her mouth on the back of her hand.

"The cottage?"

Candy nodded. "I didn't...well, until you came along I didn't spend time in here."

"Because of the former residents?"

"Yeah and it's so sad they didn't know Katya and the others were so close by."

"You said he was an old man. Maybe he couldn't have walked all that way."

"I'm sure you're right. I do still prefer sleeping in the barn when I'm on my own but if you stay...Will you?"

"I have to get back and you must come with me."

"Must?"

"Candy, you can't stay here on your own forever."

"But I'm not alone, am I? Just two days walk away is another community."

"But what if you hurt yourself? No one will come to help you. You can't stay."

"Aaron, this is my home. Yes, I'm still getting used to it and the house and the previous occupants and all that but my plants are growing.."

"And you could kill a lamb to eat."

"No!"

"But that's why farmers keep animals."

"I know but I can't kill them."

"Right."

"Not because I can't kill an animal but I can't kill these animals. They've become my friends. When I travel with Katya to the Trading, I will ask her about farming. Maybe I could raise pigs."

"And you could kill those?"

"I don't know, maybe or perhaps men would come from her valley and help me, in return for meat for themselves."

"Perhaps."

"I can manage here."

"But why do you want to?"

"Come and see."

The rain stopped and the sky cleared as they stepped through the front door. Candy pulled Aaron by the hand and they walked down towards the river. She stopped, turning round as the sun dipped below the hill spreading pink and lilac waves across the sky. She kept looking up as she turned towards the river, seeking the moon. Baas came from the hills around them and bird song rang out

The Standing Stone – The Gathering

through the trees as they neared the river bank where they sat.

"I was alone for a long time," said Candy, "Alone and frustrated with no one to talk to. I barely remember my mother, my birth mother, so I've little to go on as far as good company is concerned but Anna lied to me and Artie. They told me I was free but took away my choices. After all those years in the Dome alone, don't you think I have a right to choose how and where I live? Don't I have the right to live free beneath this beautiful sky?"

"I understand, I do," said Aaron, putting his arm around her shoulders, "But think of the good you can do if you come back. I told you, I'll be working on the plants you brought. We can find a cure for the sickness together."

Candy shook her head. "It doesn't work like that. The Talisieni council or Elders or whatever they are called will decide my fate. They won't listen."

"I'll make them," insisted Aaron.

Candy lay her head on his shoulder and he held her closer as they watched the swallows diving the length of the river, catching insects. An owl hooted in the distance as the sky darkened. "I wish you would stay. We could go to the Trading together."

"Won't you ride Afon?"

"We can take turns."

Aaron shook his head. "I need to get back."

"If you felt truly free, you wouldn't say that."

"What do you mean?"

"Well, what compels you? You were ejected from the Dome and then Anna and the scientists insist you find me. Where are 'you' in all that? Why can't you stay and make your life here?"

"Oh, Candy," he said, pulling her to him and hugging her tightly.

She could feel his heart beating fast against her neck but she said no more. She would not return to the Dome whatever he said and she would defend herself, if necessary, if others came to find her. This place was not the Badland, though she had little doubt that there had been an explosion and terrible suffering and sickness, as she had been shown by the goddess of the moon but this was her home now, whatever anyone said. Her place wasn't in the Dome or in the villages or she wouldn't have felt so compelled to escape. She had promised she would fight for the people of the earth and she would keep her vow.

The following day dawned chilly and bright. It was decided that a second boat should be completed before anyone attempted to traverse the river for suitable trees for the defensive fence so, while the Boat people, and those they were training, were busy on the river bank, the women constructed the weaving house. The wall panels were soon in place and coating of them begun but as the heat from the sun grew, the mud dried too quickly so work was abandoned in favour of roof construction. Using the materials at their disposable, straw was sewn into long mats while reeds were plaited into squares.

The Standing Stone – The Gathering

Gorse was cut from the other side of the hill and dragged to the village where it was kept dry, ready to go between the wooden rafters and the thatch.

As the men not building the boat were watering the fields and tending to the animals, Fern, Sky and River offered to take over these tasks so the main beams for the weaving house roof could be put into place. After their third trip from the river with two buckets on a heavy wooden yoke about their necks, Fern called a break and they sat beneath a beech tree in the shade.

"There has to be a better way to get water to the field," she said, rubbing her sore shoulders.

"Leather buckets are easier than clay pots or jugs," said Sky.

"But it's not just the carrying," said Fern, laying back on the grass, "There must be a way to water the whole field."

"What are you thinking?" asked River, twisting her long black curls and knotting them on top of her head.

"Nothing really, just an idea."

"Tell us and we'll see if we can help."

"It's just that we have to walk so far down the river bank to get the water to start with," said Fern, "when the field is here, on this side of the village. If there was a way down to the water and we could somehow, bring it up, that would save a lot of leg work!"

"And the new field is being cleared and that's even further away!"

"Let's explore now," said Sky, getting up, "Let's see if we can find another way down to the river."

The girls began by trying to reach the river at the point the original field ended and the new one began but as they emerged through the scrub and trees, the drop to the river was sheer.

"The river is too narrow here anyway and flows too fast," said Fern, "We should walk back and try further along."

Trees blocked their way as they tried to descend on a track adjacent to the new field but they persevered until the ground levelled and they found themselves on a river bank, similar in size to where the boats were being built. They sat with their feet in the water, talking about the possibilities until movement in the trees to their left, silenced their thinking. Flat on their stomachs, hearts racing they watched the trees. Fern was sure it was warriors but quietened her mind. They couldn't have passed the Boat people without being seen. Bracken beneath the trees moved again and laughter reached their ears before Mara appeared running towards them with Adalbern behind her. He caught her arm and pulled her to him, pressing his mouth to hers while her hands reached for his face. They collapsed into the grass. In silence, the young women slithered on their stomachs away from the riverbank until they were in the cover of trees, where they ran.

They emerged onto the field to find the men wondering where they were and though Fern explained they had been following an idea to water their crops more efficiently, the men scolded them, picking up the buckets and trudging off to fetch more water. By the

The Standing Stone – The Gathering

time the young women had returned to the village and Fern had found Nia sewing straw into mats, some of her anger had dissipated.

"We were trying to help the whole village!"

"But the men see the job and the need to get it done".

"So do we but if there's a better way, a way that will sustain us in the future..."

"I understand, Fern, but you should have completed your task first."

"We were exhausted!" said River, "If we can find a better way, all the village can help, not just the strongest men!"

"Help get this roof finished," said Nia, "Tell me your idea while we work."

Though some of the panels needed more mud, by the end of the day, the weaving house had a roof. Inside, extra branches were inserted and gorse packed between them and the thatch, while the reed woven squares were used where the mats met or in places where the straw was thinner. Layers of mats were needed to keep out the rain but this first thin layer was a start. The men returned from working on the boat and the fields to find food had only just been started and they grumbled as they drank from the beer jugs while the women cooked the stew and the flat bread.

Fern, River and Sky did not discuss seeing Mara and Adalbern. Fern knew her friends well and was sure that they realised that a commitment between the Boat people and the Tall folk may not be best for their tribe.

They were the original settlers on the land but if the Boat people and Tall folk joined forces, their ways and their traditions might be brought to the fore. Peace between the three tribes suited all at the moment but what if others sought to join them? Fern wondered how much Adalwin knew of his father's intentions.

As they sat around the fire, eating their meal, Mara, Adalbern, Geirr and Adalbern's entourage joined them. Fern met Mara's eye but the painted woman looked away, pulling Adalbern to her and kissing him full on the lips before looking back at Fern.

Once the children were settled and most of the adults had gone to bed, Fern sat beside Nia on the opposite side of the fire to Mara and Adalbern.

"What is she doing?"

"Mara? Sealing her future."

"What do you mean?"

"She would have taken Adalwin, you know but she knew you were too powerful."

"She would have taken Adalwin because she wanted him?"

"And because she thought at first she could. I was wrong about Adalwin, Fern and I'm sorry. His feelings for you are strong, I see that now and he is kind and gentle and if you are happy with him, I have no objections."

"Thank you," said Fern, putting her head on Nia's shoulder, "But if this union takes place between Mara and his father, will he be able to remain loyal to us?"

"Why not?"

The Standing Stone – The Gathering

"If Mara bears a child..."

"But Adalhard is the eldest and then Adalwin so there are two of them who can lead the tribe..."

"But their mother is not living."

"And she would have been the one to vouch for them as leader?"

"Yes," said Fern, "I asked Geirr about it."

"So your concern is that when Adalbern is gone, Mara will put her child forward?"

"Yes, and in the meantime, lead the tribe herself."

"You have thought on this, Fern."

"Anything that threatens the peace and well being of our village is worth my thought."

"But the Tall Folk will not accept her," said Nia, "They do not know her like they do Adalhard and Adalwin."

"But Mara has gold." Fern whispered the final word.

"She gave us tokens but..."

"I suggested she hid her treasure, somewhere the village would not dare to go."

Nia turned to Fern, her eyes wide open and a small smile on her face. "But you would?"

Fern nodded. "There is more gold. Enough to bribe greedy villagers."

"What will you do?"

"Nothing," said Fern, "but I will be vigilant."

Early in the morning, work on the weaving house walls began. To ensure its slow drying, they hung skins over the new panels. Fern found Geirr and asked him to come with her down to the river bank. Following an accident, Lugh, Mara's brother, was confined to constructing paddles in the shade and his twisted, splinted ankle lay out in front of him. He scowled as Fern approached.

"Please translate for me Geirr," she said as they sat down on the mud beside Lugh, "How is your ankle feeling?"

Lugh shrugged not taking his eyes from his work. He had allowed Nia and Fern to treat his ankle as no one of their tribe knew how to straighten it but he still treated Fern with contempt.

"We need your advice."

Lugh stopped his sanding and looked up.

"You have more experience of water than we do. As the village grows, we need more crops and the walk with water from the river to the fields is a long one. I have an idea and I wondered if I could show you."

Lugh's face remained impassive but he gave the briefest of nods so, taking this as consent, Fern began to tell him of her ideas and drew lines in the mud. When she had finished, both men stared at her.

"How, I mean, where did you get that idea?" said Geirr, "I knew you were wise, my lady but you think with such foresight, as if you have heard these ideas before."

"How could that be, Geirr? I saw a problem and have been trying to find a solution but I cannot know if it will work. I thought Lugh might know."

"Moving water in large quantities can be done," said Lugh, his matted dreads nodding in agreement, "but the right place needs to be found. Basins to hold water will need to be lined with stones and a single post there will not be strong enough," he added, using a stick to add lines to her sketch, "but one like this would work and you are right about the shape of the bucket."

Lugh's blue eyes shone. "While there is water in the river, you could raise crops on ten fields with this, even twenty!"

"Would you help us?" asked Fern, "When your foot is better?"

Lugh rested back against the tree trunk. "My allegiance is to my sister and I miss the sea."

"Of course, I would not take you from anything Mara wanted you to do. You should tell us more of the sea, Lugh. None of my village has seen it."

Lugh nodded slowly, his eyes remaining on Fern's. "But my sister pursues her own interests. She forgets me and the sea. I will help you."

"I'm sure she does not forget. Life is different for you all now. I hope you will soon settle and feel part of this village. I am grateful for all the help you can give us. Thank you."

As Fern and Geirr walked back to the village, Geirr continued to ask her questions about the new river bank while Fern thought of Lugh's sad blue eyes and his concern for his sister and longing for the sea he loved.

"Please don't mention this to anyone, Geirr, not even Adalbern."

"Oh, I can't lie to him, my lady."

"Not lie just keep it from him a while longer. Please. Until we know for certain if this is possible, there is no point everyone getting excited. You know what everyone is like!"

Geirr laughed, his bright red ears peeling on either side of his felt hat. "Yes, I do, yes I can remain silent on this."

"Thank you. Now let me tell you of another thought I had..."

"More ideas! You will wear out your head with all this thinking, my lady!"

Chapter 8

As Rhys helped Mr Evans with the shop and deliveries, Rachel spent the first week of May on her own. As the 'sisters' raised bed was already planted, she tried something different in the other, choosing vegetables and herbs she ate every week or would like to. Leeks, carrots and beetroot were her choice and with soil and compost left over, she constructed a row of bags, sat on old tyres, in which she planted sprouting potatoes. One quarter of the raised bed was planted with herbs, rosemary, parsley and oregano.

Over two rain soaked days, busy indoors, she filled a box with bunting and another with wrapped gifts for the Lucky Dip. Mrs Williams was icing a cake for the main raffle but Rachel offered to bake it so on the first dry day in a week, Rhys entered the cottage to find the house smelling of Christmas and Rachel at the kitchen table cutting out squares from scraps of material.

"That smells good," he said, dropping his bag on the kitchen floor, "Guess we can't use your oven for a while then?"

"It'll be a few hours yet. Why?"

"I picked up some crusts from the bakery yesterday. Gave some to Mrs Jones for bread pudding and I was going to bake one for you, my special recipe. It'll be fine. I need to soak the sultanas first."

"Do you know," said Rachel, standing up, her dress making scissors in her hand, "I can't remember when I last had bread pudding. Marcus hates it...hated it."

"What are the squares for?"

"This batch are for lavender bags. I'm going to fill and machine this up and they'll go into bags the children are making at the primary school."

"Great idea to get the children involved," said Rhys, switching on the kettle.

"Beth's been so busy. I think it's the way it should be though, the whole community working together. We're running a poster competition, another of Beth's ideas called Community = Big Family but we're struggling for donations for prizes. Some of the shops have offered gift vouchers which is lovely but they don't 'look' anything on a display."

"Have you spoken to Tanwen Griffiths?" asked Rhys, pouring water into the tea pot.

"I haven't. Don't know about Beth."

"She's a writer. Lovely lady, lives with about twenty cats up on the mountain road to Sarn Helen. I'm sure she would help but she doesn't socialise much and probably doesn't know about the fund raiser."

Rachel jotted the name into her notebook. "It's getting there though," she said, "We've stalls selling food, drink and fresh produce as well as a coconut shy, Lucky Dip and even Whack a Rat!"

"That's a proper summer fayre."

Rachel consulted a list in a plastic folder. "The scouts are running a penalty shoot out to win a football and are lending us some of their plastic ducks with numbers on the bottom."

Rhys raised his eyebrows.

The Standing Stone – The Gathering

"They have an annual duck race to raise money for Wales Air Ambulance."

"And you'll use them for what?"

"They said we can screw hooks into our twenty so the children can fish them from a paddling pool with rods and string with a ring on the end."

"I'm sure I had a game like that. Magnetic fishing rods, I think they were."

"I know the game but I didn't have toys like that."

"It's great fun! What about Buckaroo? I love Buckaroo!"

Rachel laughed. "You're such a big kid."

"Who isn't? How's the veg coming along?"

"I know I planted late but that can't be helped. Pour the tea and I'll show you."

That night, as Rachel snuggled into her duvet, an image of the goddess Rhiannon and the Beltane ritual filled her mind. How could a person appear out of nowhere? At the time, on the mound with Rhys, dressed in strange clothing, out beneath the moon, calling in a goddess seemed a natural thing to do but now, in the real world, she wondered if Rhys were pandering to her. Maybe her mind was deluded, shocked by Marcus' death, seeking out safe, supportive images to sustain her. The ritual had been impromptu though and she had no idea that Rhys would ask her to call in the goddess.

What if all this, the goddesses, Candy and Fern, were all one big illusion? What difference would it make? Bringing the gods and goddesses and the world of

Nature into her life could only be beneficial, whatever her religious or spiritual beliefs. That was another question to think on. What did she believe and why? Neither of her parents had any religious leanings, though their wedding had been a lavish, Church of England affair. She had been christened, she had the cups, money boxes and silver spoons to prove it but had no inkling as to who her god parents might be.

Wide awake, Rachel went down to the kitchen and made hot chocolate in the microwave while the kettle boiled for a hot water bottle. She enjoyed the silent night in the cottage, safe with her thoughts, allowing ideas to develop in her mind without retort.

Back in bed she felt warmer, closing her eyes as she revisited her limited religious experiences. At school, there was Harvest Festival and Christmas but none of the other, older festivals were celebrated. She remembered a May Day holiday but only knew now that it was akin to Beltane. School assemblies had been about pretending to sing while paying as little attention as possible and her RE lessons were solely based on Christian Old and New Testament teaching. Children of minority religious persuasions sat in the corridor during assembly and Rachel realised, she knew nothing about them or their beliefs.

As the hot water bottle lulled her and the warm milk soothed, Rachel fell asleep with the image of Binah standing on a mountain top with Ishtar and Rhiannon beside her, looking down on the specks of civilisation below.

The Standing Stone – The Gathering

The morning dawned bright but chill. Candy left Aaron sleeping in the barn while she walked down to the river. Pink mist rose from the water to greet her. Boots off, she sat down. Fluff the lamb nudged her in the back before skittering away with her sister, Cloud, to explore the river bank. As the cool water refreshed her feet she realised that the land following the river downstream was unexplored by her, as was the land across it. Climbing the hills, looking for her neighbours had consumed her time and thoughts while she had neglected to seek out new people along the river. After the Trading, she would explore more of the countryside, maybe finding more agreeable neighbours. As the sun warmed the wispy clouds away, she washed her face. She traced the lines of her face with a finger, exploring the contours as she gazed into the shimmering mirror. Freckles spattered her nose but her skin was bronzed. A worried face stared back at her, soon breaking into a grin as Fluff bumped into her, fleeing from her sister. They walked back up to the cottage.

Afon greeted her from his stable and she led him out to the field with the nosy sheep. Katya had said that the grass in the valley was very rich and Afon was not to eat too much of it but Candy wanted him to feel happy in his new home so she let him explore. She made a full circuit of the field, noting where the hedgerows were thin in places and where fence posts needed replacing. With her trusty bill hook, she filled the worst holes with dead twigs and small branches. For a more permanent solution, there were pointed posts in a lean-to at the end of the barn but she wasn't sure how she would bang them into place. Afon contentedly nibbled the grass, as Candy shut the large gate, preventing him from wandering down to the river. The adjacent small wooden gate led into her garden.

The plants in her green house were thriving and she spent an hour watering and with her hands in the earth, pulling out brambles and digging out stones. Every day she cleared a little more, methodically extending her planting area without needing to bother Aaron. As her shoulders grew tired she wished he would stay, adding his commitment to a new life for them both. It would be easier together as each lent their strengths to the task of making a home and feeding themselves, but she knew he was pulled by his father to return to the Dome.

When Aaron found her in the garden, she was using a sharpening stone on a pair of hand shears.

"Morning! You look dreadful! I've lit the fire in the cottage. Stoke it up and put some water on for tea."

"You been up long?" said Aaron, pushing back his hair from his face before stretching into a yawn.

"Yeah, long time. The weather's warming up so I thought we could make a start on shearing the sheep."

"You know how?"

Candy laughed. "No, but how hard can it be?"

A weak smile broke on Aaron's tired face. "A hot drink and some breakfast should wake me up. Just couldn't stay asleep last night."

"You looked flat out this morning. The biscuit mix is covered with a cloth. Make some for me too."

The Standing Stone – The Gathering

They decided to shear between the barn and the two dilapidated sheds but they needed a plan to gather the sheep together. A stack of metal hurdles discovered under some sacking in the barn made an enclosure but the two of them found it difficult to herd the sheep.

"We need a dog," said Aaron, red faced and sweating.

"Maybe but I wonder if Afon could help?"

"You're going to round up sheep on horseback?"

"It's worth a try, don't you think?"

Aaron stood with his hands on his hips, smiling at her, his blue eyes prominent in his tanned chiselled face.

"What?"

"Nothing beats you, does it?"

"I don't give up, if that's what you mean."

"But you have no idea how to live like this."

"So? I'm learning. I'd have to learn to live anywhere, wouldn't I? After the Dome, living life and being free is a blessing. I intend to embrace it."

"Do you think you can ride Afon?"

"Won't know until I try."

Afon nuzzled her as she approached him in the field and she stroked his neck, talking to him gently as she ran her hands over his back. She told him about the sheep, how hot they were in their woolly coats and how she needed to gather them so they could be shorn. Afon turned his head, looking into her eyes and snorting gently, his ears wiggling forward and then back, as she explained her plan to him. While Aaron stayed by the sheep pen, Candy pulled herself across Afon's back and hung there a while, letting him get used to her weight.

He stamped his feet a little and shifted about but as Candy eased herself into a sitting position, holding onto the soft halter, he stood still, lifting his head as she turned him towards the top of the field.

Once at the furthest end, Afon and Candy rode across the field back and forth easing the sheep down in front of them. Aaron had doubled the size of the entrance to the holding pen so as the sheep gathered momentum in front of the horse and rider, pushed closer to the hedge, the group narrowed to single file, towards the pen. While Aaron stood to one side, hanging onto a long rope attached to the gate, Afon and Candy walked slowly down, trickling the sheep into the waiting pen. Once inside, Aaron secured the gate with only two renegades escaping so by the time the sun was at its zenith, more than fifty sheep and lambs were ready for shearing.

Candy thanked Afon as she dismounted. He tossed his head and resumed eating grass while in the pen, Aaron tried to catch a sheep to shear. After four attempts, Candy was crying with laughter.

"Funny? Ha? Your turn then."

As with Aaron, as Candy entered the pen, the sheep veered away from her. She chose a young female and watched the way she moved, how she dipped her head to try to disappear in the pack. Talking gently, she moved towards the sheep, cut right to cut off her exit to the pack and steered her towards the double hurdle arrangement they had made. With a plank of wood behind her, the sheep was keen to move forward when the second hurdle was removed and as she set foot in the yard, Candy took hold of her around the neck and shoulders and pulled her towards her, landing the sheep on her back. The sheep let out a long baa and relaxed. Aaron handed Candy the shears.

"How did you do that? I mean, how did you know how?"

"I didn't. I just thought about the sheep and me and what I wanted to do and how it would help her. I tried to reassure her that she wouldn't be hurt and then went for it. Look at her feet too," she added, "We need to get those other small clippers sharpened. These bits of nail are all bent over. Must be really uncomfortable."

Aaron laughed. "So you're not only giving haircuts but pedicures too!"

Candy glared at him. "I presume you mean nail cutting and yes, of course! How would you like to walk around all day on your own toe nails!"

"You're right. I'll find the clippers."

As the sun began to near the horizon, twenty sheep had been relieved of their winter coats. The fleeces weren't pretty and there were additional chunks in the heap but it was a warm, useful pile of wool. There was water in the holding pen but the remaining sheep couldn't stay there. Letting them go back into the field behind the house would entail another morning rounding them up again so while Aaron cooked bacon on the outdoor fire and potatoes from Katya in the embers, Candy walked the perimeter of the smaller field beside the house. There were a few places in need of repair but she bundled fallen branches and twigs into the gaps as the light began to fail. They set up a row of hurdles to funnel the sheep into the field and let them into their new home by the light of Aaron's lantern.

In her blanket poncho, exhausted and dirty, Candy devoured her bacon and potato and looked up to see Aaron smiling at her. "I'll eat yours if you're not hungry," she said.

"No way!" laughed Aaron, moving his plate, "Happy?"

"Of course," said Candy, putting down her empty plate and stretching her arms, "Tired but happy."

"And this is what you want?"

"Living here? Of course. This is my home. These are my animals and my land. I am responsible for them and in return, they will help me. You enjoyed it too."

Aaron nodded. "I did, you're right and I wouldn't have wanted to miss you and Afon herding the sheep."

"So stay," said Candy, "There's two bed frames up in the rafters, did you see them? I'm thinking of moving the small bed out, maybe use it for something else. I can't see me ever sleeping in it and we could rearrange that end of the cottage."

"I can't stay," said Aaron.

"But you want to," said Candy, leaning into him.

He kissed the top of her head. "I know."

Council was called and agreed to the building of a new house to smoke fish and meat. Fern's village had grown and changed in the space of a few months as the three

The Standing Stone – The Gathering

tribes worked to live together as one community. Not only could more crops be planted in the new fields but they were learning how to get the best yields from their harvest and how best to store and preserve it. With everyone able practising with bow and arrow, hunting parties contained women and young adults for the first time, though often the weapon of preference was a spear. Without work to occupy them, the men would have been unhappy as their hunting role was usurped but their skills and strength were needed for other tasks, clearing trees, digging over the land, building boats and watering the crops.

Now able to put weight on his foot, Lugh led a group of men and boys clearing a wide track way down to the river, adjacent to the new field. Fresh nettles were harvested for soup by the women while Fern and her friends made a new cart of small branches, capable of moving firewood back to the village. River had found the tree disc, already rotten in the middle so once they had gouged it out and added an axle and two shafts, it could be pulled easily across the bumpy ground.

Four dry bright days were followed by four days of wet, squally weather. Work outside was unpleasant so they lit fires in their houses and while the women applied themselves to making mittens or fabric, the young girls spun for them or made baskets to carry their wares to the Gathering.

As Fern completed another basket, a flash and rumble from the sky set the babies crying and she rose to calm them as Adalwin pulled back the skin opening and greeted her with a wet hug. He hung his cape by the door and followed her to the fire, taking a weeping toddler onto his lap to pacify him. Another flash pierced the gloom and some of the women cried out as a shattering crack rumbled the earth beneath them. Two of the Olds began to chant and rock, tears streaming from their eyes as Fern walked among her people, trying to soothe their worries. She knelt to a tousled head, hiding beneath a bench and Hugh sprang into her arms where she rocked him and wiped away his tears. Men and women sat together around the fire and Fern heard words like 'bad omens' and 'upsetting the gods' spreading through her house.

She stood on one of the benches. "My people, there is nothing to fear. We know that in nature, there is balance. Cold and hot, wet and dry and this is the way that the sky balances nature. We have been warm in a cloudless sky these past four days but we saw the clouds gathering yesterday. We were hot last night and it was hard to breath easy but now, this storm will drive away the clouds and bring rain and coolness to our sleep. Feel how the air lightens."

She lifted her arms as the first raindrops began to hit the roof, tapping at first before pouring down onto the thatch. Chill air seeped into the house and the tension of the storm left it. As the mood in the house lifted and men and women resumed their making, Fern took Adalwin's hand and they walked out into the rain together.

"I need to find Nia," said Fern, looking at Adalwin, "Have you seen her?"

Adalwin shook his head. "With Geirr perhaps?"

With Adalwin's cloak of skin over them, they trudged through mud towards Adalbern's long house. Though chilled by the new fresh breeze, Fern was blissfully warm with Adalwin's arm around her. She turned to him as they neared the entrance and he pulled her closer, his lips finding hers as she let out a moan of pleasure. Adalwin smiled at her and she blushed as they walked into the crowded long house.

Mara and Adalbern sat together on a raised platform while all around them sat men and a few women, drinking and laughing. Geirr sat beside Mara, translating her words while Adalbern stared at her, one hand on her thigh and the other holding his drinking horn. Fern squeezed Adalwin's hand as they approached. She knew the power of words and she sensed Mara too knew how to use them.

"Ah, my son, come and join us," called Adalbern, as they neared the centre of the room.

"We're looking for Nia," said Fern, "Thank you but I must find her."

"Son, come and drink with me," said Adalbern, ignoring Fern, "You must sit here with us."

"Come on," laughed Mara, "Or am I not woman enough for both of you!"

The men laughed and Adalbern kissed Mara's cheek and pulled her too him.

"We seek Nia," said Adalwin, "Have you seen her?"

"I saw her this morning, on her way to the mound," said Geirr, "but it's been raining hard for many hours. She must be in her house."

"We've just come from there," said Fern, "but thank you, I will go to the mound."

"Stay Adalwin," said Mara, "Your father wants you to stay, don't you Adalbern?"

"I must help Fern find Nia," said Adalwin, in his own tongue, "She cannot go alone."

"Then when you find her, you will come back here," said Adalbern, "I want you with me."

"As you wish, father," said Adalwin, bowing as he walked backwards a few paces before striding towards the door.

The rain had eased to a light drizzle and a watery sun was fighting through the remaining cloud. Steam rose from the houses in the village as Fern and Adalwin slipped through the mud towards the path to the mound. Fern stopped to catch her breath. She turned to Adalwin, noting the furrow in his brow and redness of his cheeks.

"I should not keep you from your father."

"We must find Nia," said Adalwin, his mouth tightening, "I...I am sick with them, all of them. Even when no rain falls, they sit and drink and laugh and are of no use. All else work, why not them?"

"Your father has a difficult job. He must make decisions for the whole tribe."

"But all men can cut trees, clear land and water crops because all men want to eat."

"I know but your women make wonderful cloth and this will be sold at the Gathering to help provide food, salt and animals for all."

Adalwin shook his head. "Your tribe works for others. Our women make for father."

"No, you are wrong. Adalbern agreed at council. As your tribe needed help with food to begin with, they will pay back with trades they make in cloth."

"I hear father talking with Mara. He promises her much."

"But she knows my village provided for her tribe. She would not take from us."

"She will not give either."

Fern grabbed Adalwin's arm. "True?"

"Yes, true," said Adalwin.

"But can't she see we will survive best if we work together? She must see, she is wise."

"Others work, she takes," spat Adalwin, "She thinks of herself, not others."

"We must find Nia," said Fern, pushing on up the path, "She will know what to do."

They began calling Nia as they neared the summit of the mound and continued as they walked to the barrows but there was no response. From the top of the mound they called again.

"Wait," said Fern.

She traced the narrow path down between two rocks and disappeared from Adalwin's view. Between two more rocks, down a slope and between two more, Fern stepped under the shade of a weeping willow tree and knelt at the sacred pool. Her heart pounded in her ears and her stomach twisted as she tried to calm herself to ask her question. She took a deep breath and let it out slowly. With her left hand on her heart, she placed her right hand in the water and waited until her head stopped buzzing.

She stirred the water with her right hand before showering her face with the droplets, letting them fall onto her closed eyelids. She opened them and looked into the pool. She saw Nia, lying wet and muddy and calmed herself again as she looked for clues as to where she was. Pulling back from the picture, she saw a carved wooden oar against a tree.

Aled and Belle ran with Adalwin and Fern to the river bank. They found Nia in a hollow, near the water's edge, where she had slipped down the bank. A basket lay beside her, full of herbs and watercress. Her arm was turned awkwardly beneath her. Before she would let them move Nia, Fern touched all over Nia's body as she had seen her do after one of the village children took a hard fall. Nia did not flinch to any of her touches so, apart from her arm, there didn't seem to be any other serious injury.

Adalwin carried Nia back to her house while Fern called her name and tried to rouse her. Even moving her off her arm had not woken Nia and Fern feared this was the ending sleep. While Adalwin went to his father, Fern and Belle stripped Nia of her wet clothes as gently as they could, dried her and wrapped her to get warm. Fern

The Standing Stone – The Gathering

knew to do this slowly. She tried to force water between Nia's lips but it trickled out so holding back her tears, Fern lifted Nia's arm onto the top of the covers. Nia whimpered and the women hugged each other before soothing Nia as they splinted her arm. They fixed the upper arm and then the lower before binding the two so Nia's arm was set across her chest. Fern hoped she was doing as Nia would have done but with no one to ask, she acted with authority and Belle left to find the soothing willow bark to ease the pain.

Nia's body trembled as if cold but her forehead was hot and her cheeks flushed. Fern recognised the first signs of fever so when Belle came back, she instructed her to move the people from the house and find them shelter with other families. Belle's face was wide eyed with questions and Fern hugged her. They looked at Nia.

"I will look after her," said Fern, "The goddess will guide me but she will get worse, I know it. We must hope she then gets well. Will you take Rowan with you, please?"

"Of course. She and Bramble can help start on the food." She picked up Nia's basket. "We must not waste this," she added, her voice trembling, "Nia would be furious."

"Thank you. Tell the village I call Council. I will be there when the sun drops below the hill."

"Nia fell by the river before the storm today," said Fern, "and she has a fever."

The hut was full of villagers while others hung around outside the door. A murmur of worry ran through the crowd.

"I shall speak for her, as you know I can. We must all work together to finish the weaving hut for Mara's people and continue our work, at every opportunity, to clear the new field and start piling firewood."

"What about the work on the river bank?" called a voice from the back of the hut, "Should we continue now it is raining again?"

"Stick with the groups you have been working in," said Fern, "Geirr, will you help move the groups around like we were doing before? Three days on one task and then move to another."

"If my lord Adalbern has no need of me," said Geirr, looking to Adalbern.

Mara spoke into Adalbern's ear before he answered. "I have need of Geirr," said Adalbern, "He needs to oversee packing of the cloth and deciding value. I cannot spare him."

"I see," said Fern, "Celyn, will you look after the working groups?"

"I will, Fern," said Celyn, "but we need more hands in the new field. It's back breaking work and though we take breaks to bring in firewood, each day we work slower."

"Will your men help in the new field, Adalbern?"

"We gather firewood and practise our archery skills for the safety of the village. You want more?" His face was blotchy and his nose red as he slurred the words for Geirr to translate while Mara whispered in his ear.

"And how will your tribe be fed next year if we don't turn this land for growing?" asked Fern.

Adalbern stood and walked towards Fern, towering over the villagers. "We make cloth to sell for our food, woman. We will not be wanting."

"And you'll transport enough food back from the Gathering to feed your whole tribe?"

Adalbern glanced quickly at Mara before roaring his response. "I don't need a woman telling me how to feed my people!"

"But we've all helped making the cloth," insisted Fern, "It's worth should be shared between all three tribes. We support each other."

"Our women make cloth. It is ours to sell for its worth."

Whispers in the hut soon turned to cries of outrage as Adalbern, with Mara on his arm, pushed through the crowd towards the door.

"Council is not closed!" cried Fern, "Not all has been decided."

Adalbern turned on her, his blood shot eyes staring down as he spat out his words. "I have decided!"

Mara stepped away from Adalbern. "I speak for all the Boat People. We make boats to fetch wood to protect the village and to bring in more wood for building and burning. These are our tasks while Adalbern protects and provides for us."

"But we built the weaving house for you! We took you in and gave you food. We nursed your mothers and babies, giving you time to settle in our village."

"We don't need your weaving house," said Mara, "We don't want to live with you. Adalbern has given us shelter so we will not trouble you further."

"Why are you doing this?" said Fern, looking to Geirr. He translated.

Mara shrugged her shoulders, her dreadlocks bouncing from her head. "I do nothing but honour this great man. He will provide for us."

"But you're dividing the village, it cannot work."

Mara stood tall and looked down on Fern. "You speak as if it's your village and that you should decide its fate. It suits your village to use the Boat People and the Tall Folk for their skills while your tribe scrapes pathetically at the soil and tends a few thin animals!"

Laughter rippled around the hut but was halted as Adalwin moved to stand beside Fern. "Father, Fern's village helped us as she said and she was the one who stopped you attacking the Boat People. We need to work together. What if the warriors attack?"

Murmurs of approval rose around Fern and men stood around Adalwin but Mara laughed and Adalbern joined her. They were still laughing as they left the Council hut.

Chapter 9

With just two weeks to go before the Midsummer fayre, Rachel heard Rhys calling as she pegged out a line of clothes.

"I was right," he said, following her into the kitchen.

"About what?"

"The clothes on the line. All work clothes. It's time you had a day off."

Rachel laughed. "I don't need a day off."

"So you don't want to go for a picnic on the beach?"

"With you?"

"What's wrong with me?"

"Nothing, I just...I don't know."

"So, do you fancy it?"

"I don't know."

Rhys turned round in the small space left by the plastic boxes in the kitchen and began to walk out.

"Where are you going? I've just put the kettle on."

She watched his gentle face tinged with sadness as it struggled for words. Though blond haired, his skin was a healthy light brown and though his jawline and cheekbones were still chiselled, he had lost that angular slightly bony look.

"I'm going to the beach. I made us a picnic and was hoping you would be excited to go but I'll not waste a beautiful day arguing and I'm certainly not begging you to come."

"Okay, if it makes you happy."

"No, don't you dare come to please me!"

"Rhys, I'm sorry. I'd planned my day, that's all but it can keep. Really, it's a great idea and I bet you know some great beaches."

Rhys shuffled his feet and looked down at his boots. "If you're sure."

"I am. Let me go and change and throw a few bits in a bag. Do you need anything to go with the picnic? I bought more ginger beer. It's in the fridge."

"Thank you. That would be lovely."

They set off in the muddy Land Rover, Rachel wondering how so much mud could get on the inside of a car. Snaking across country through narrow winding lanes, the land soon dropped down and once they had crossed the main coast road, they headed towards the beach.

"You alright?" asked Rachel.

"Yeah, sorry, it's just sometimes..."

"I'm hard to get out of the house?"

"No, well..."

"I'm hard to excite?"

"No, yes..."

"I'm difficult to please?"

Rhys laughed. "All the above, to be honest. I was just gutted you didn't love the idea, that's all."

"Sorry and you're right. Going out is still an effort because I feel safe at home. I'm sorry I stole your thunder."

They pulled into a lay-by at the side of the road and Rhys pulled a large rucksack from the back seat. Two fold up chairs in bags and a fold up table went over his shoulders before he picked up the bag of ginger beer and bottles of water.

"I can manage those," said Rachel, taking them from him, "What on earth is in there?"

"Picnic," grinned Rhys.

The walk down to the beach was a steep but short one and as the tide was going out, an expanse of fresh clean sand emerged as the sun grew stronger. By the time they had walked to a section of cliffs with amazing rock formations, it was a perfect summer's day. A glowing orange circle hung in a cloudless blue sky above the gentle rolling ocean as Rhys set up the camping table and chairs and a sumptuous picnic.

They ate prawns, crusty French bread and salad and sipped chilled ginger beer, watching the water lapping onto the beach.

"This is lovely, Rhys. I'm so glad you suggested it."

"You deserve a break," said Rhys, smiling as he produced a Brie and a bunch of red grapes from a cool bag in his rucksack.

Rachel was glad she had brought her wide brimmed straw hat as the sun grew hotter. She felt herself dozing in her chair as the healing warmth of the sun soothed her aching muscles. With the picnic and table packed away, they adjourned to a blanket, using their hoodies as pillows.

"You're right," said Rachel, wriggling her toes as a gentle breeze off the sea cooled them. "I do deserve this."

Rhys lay beside her, taking her hand, his thumb gently caressing her fingers. "I wanted to do something special for you. I don't make many new friends, certainly none as beautiful as you, so I wanted to let you know, you see, how much you are appreciated."

She squeezed his hand and he brought it to his lips and kissed it.

A quiver began in Rachel's stomach and ran down her legs. All her aches dissipated and the heady sea air and healing properties of the sun intoxicated her as she rolled on her side to face Rhys.

He smiled at her, pushing back a stray strand of dark hair, blown loose by the wind. "Happy?"

"Relaxed," smiled Rachel, shutting her eyes, her hat falling back onto the blanket.

Feather light kisses caressed her forehead. Surprise thrilled her but she lay motionless as he kissed her cheek and chin, before brushing lightly on her parted lips. Her eyes remained closed as Rhys' lips remained on hers. He pressed closer as she kissed him back. And then he was gone.

She tried to open her eyes but the sun was too bright and she turned, fumbling for her hat before sitting up to find Rhys taking off his cotton shirt.

"You fancy a swim?" he asked, standing up.

"I'm okay," said Rachel, shielding her eyes as she tried to discern his facial expression. "I might paddle in a bit."

"I'll look out for you," he said, smiling.

The Standing Stone – The Gathering

She watched him, or rather the taut shape his bottom made in his swimming shorts, as he walked towards the water before laying back on the blanket and closing her eyes. Her mind whirred frantically, desperate to make a case for why Rhys had kissed her. Was the picnic part of the seduction? Was there more to come? She bit her lip, tears prickling her eyes. It was a beautiful kiss and in that warm, mellow place she had kissed him back when deep down, she knew with certainty, that she loved Rhys as a friend and not a lover.

She stood in the shallows, the water kissing her toes as Rhys swam and rolled in the ocean. The gentle swell of the water's proceed and retreat were the only sound as peace descended on her and concerns about their friendship left her. Once out of the water, he chased her, dripping wet, threatening to hug her and Rachel knew her Rhys was back. There were no attempts at intimate seduction as they spent the afternoon finishing the Brie, grapes and bread before clouds across the sun began to chill the air. Rhys dropped her home with a smile and a kiss on the cheek.

The following evening, she and Rhys watched a movie together but no mention was made of the kiss on the beach. Rhys was his kind, attentive, funny self and Rachel hugged him when it was time for bed. He slept on the sofa, as he often did and while she was in the kitchen making porridge the following morning, he opened the door to an armful of roses.

"I didn't know you had company," said Oliver, handing Rachel the flowers.

"My car disappeared, has it?" said Rhys, stepping out onto the drive, "No, seems to be there."

"I came to bring you these and donations for the Midsummer fayre," said Oliver, ignoring Rhys and opening a huge canvas bag that hung on his arm. "I've more prizes for your Lucky Dip and I thought this may be suitable for one of the main raffle prizes."

He handed Rachel a top of the range bread maker.

"Wow!" said Rachel, "That's so kind of you. Oliver, do you know Rhys?"

"Of course," said Oliver, smirking, "He's the delivery boy."

"I'm helping out Mr Evans," said Rhys.

"Of course you are. Rachel, I came to see if you needed help. It's only a few weeks until the fayre."

Oliver stood close to her in the kitchen as she arranged her flowers in a vase.

"We're just having breakfast and I always make too much. Will you join us?"

"I only had juice this morning," said Oliver, "I'd love to. Have you tried juicing?" he continued, "The vitamins you get in one glass of juice would take you an hour to eat if you had to devour the whole fruits and vegetables."

"Shall we eat in the garden?" asked Rhys, "It's warming up."

"Yes, let's."

"I'll sort the table," said Rhys.

"And I will take your flowers to go on it," said Oliver.

Once both men had left the kitchen, Rachel sat down on a chair with a bump. What on earth was going on now? Two men fighting for her attention before 10am on a Saturday morning was a totally new experience and she knew it was naughty of her but she was really enjoying it. As she carried three bowls of porridge, brown sugar and three coffees on a tray into the garden, she skipped lightly down the path, imagining herself a sweet young damsel, fought over by the knight's of King Arthur's court.

The lateness of her planting severely limited her harvest but two rescued courgette plants were thriving as were the strawberry plants Candy had salvaged from the long grass. The extra netting added to the flimsy fence was rusty but seemed to have kept the rabbits out. She had caught a glimpse of the vegetable gardens in Katya's valley and was keen to gain more knowledge about growing in her own garden.

"If only I had goods for the Trading," she told Aaron, as they ate onion, courgette and tomatoes from the pan with a fork. "Or even something to barter with at Katya's house. These tomatoes are delicious!"

"But you'll not need new plants," said Aaron.

"I will," insisted Candy, "I need to plant in the autumn to get year round food but most of all, I need goods to barter for grain. Flour for our biscuits is nearly gone and I want to make bread. Until the potatoes come in, it's our only staple."

"You can't possibly survive here."

"Of course I can!"

"But how are you going to make anything to barter?"

"Shut up! It's always 'can't' with you!"

She jumped to her feet and threw her fork at him.

"Hey!"

"You deserve it! I know you're going back because you don't want to live here but stop telling me what I can and can't do! Just go! Go back to your father and leave me alone!"

She ran down the hill towards the river, a gibbous moon lighting her way. As the fresh clean sound of water rushing downstream rose up to meet her, Candy's anger diminished and tears prickled her eyes. For so much of her life she had been alone. There had been no one to talk to or listen to or even sit in the same room with and yet now, with another free human in such close proximity, negative words, excuses and disagreement were all she and Aaron could manage.

With the lack of rainfall this past two weeks, the river was low. Stones appeared she hadn't seen before and without a thought she stepped across them to the other side of the water. She walked a little way downstream until the river widened. When she couldn't see her feet, she sat down, facing her riverbank.

She had no concept in her mind of a hard life, not after the Dome. Any life where she could talk, laugh and sing and have an opinion could not be hard. Her needs were minimal because she had owned nothing before. Now she had a cottage, a barn, buildings, a garden, land,

The Standing Stone – The Gathering

a horse and sheep so how could she not think a happy life was possible with so many blessings? All she needed to do was think of something to take to the Trading and she trusted she would think of it but the first new moon had passed. She had just over three weeks before she needed to set off.

A familiar baa sounded on the opposite bank followed by another. Two faces appeared out of the murk and baaed in unison making Candy laugh. She chuckled to herself as she picked her way along the bank to the stones shining in the river, and crossed to be greeted by Fluff and Cloud. They walked back to the cottage.

Aaron was not by the fire but Candy saw a light in the cottage which was quickly extinguished. She turned away, lit her lantern hanging on the barn door and went to check on Afon. He greeted her warmly, nuzzling her hair and accepting the last of Katya's carrots. She was patting him, hugging his neck as Aaron appeared in the door way.

"I'm sorry," said Aaron, "I'd forgotten about your life in the Dome."

She shook her head. "I try to forget and being here helps but not when you're all ...sensible."

"I just worry about you, that's all. I just think you'll be better off with other people, using your skills, making a difference."

"I want to make my own choices and use my skills, as you put it, in my own way. You've lived in the Dome. Do you want people telling you what to do and directing your life after that?"

"My father has always been a large part of my life."

"Fair enough, he's your father so I guess you miss him."

"No," said Aaron, "You don't understand. My life in the Dome was different from yours."

Candy gave Afon a final pat. "Then tell me," she said, "We'll build up the fire and talk. If you're going back, rather than coming to the Trading, I'd like to find out a little more about you."

"Why?" He took her arm and turned her to face him.

The moonlight on his face highlighted his cheek bones and sent her eyes down to his soft full lips.

"You saved me," said Candy, taking his hand and swinging her arm as they walked back to the fire. "You're the only person who has ever really cared about me. I know it didn't work out in the village but I learned a lot there and I do miss Artie...even Ben sometimes. I enjoyed being part of their family and they made me very welcome. Why wouldn't I want to know more about The Whisperer who saved me?"

Aaron smiled and squeezed her hand. She built up the fire while he fetched water.

In his blanket poncho, Aaron talked. "Alphas are not taken from their mother if she is spared from having more children."

"You know your mother?"

Aaron nodded. "But the only way that can happen is if the father can vouch that his Alpha child will bring future worth to the Dome. I lived with my mother, was schooled with other Alphas by a tutor and my future was decreed by my father."

Candy gasped. "So because you helped me and were ejected, you've lost your mother. Aaron, I'm so sorry."

"It's not your fault, really. Anyway, I no longer lived with my mother once I had completed all the home tutor could teach. Most Alphas are schooled in a University, with both human, robot and screen tuition and that's where I went. I excelled in natural sciences. Father tried to steer me towards maths and physics. I insisted on biology as I wanted to be a doctor," said Aaron, holding his face in his hands one moment, looking away from her the next, "My father and I argued."

"What happened?"

"Mother worked within the administration of the Dome. She too was an Alpha. She and my father arranged my conception and birth as their duty to the Company. After the argument I saw neither of them for three years. I lived in the University. Friendships were not encouraged as it was felt it detracted from our studies."

Candy took his hand. "So you were alone too?"

"Yeah and the people who set me adrift were my own parents."

"I see your point," said Candy, hugging his arm. "I barely remember my mother and there never was a father. I had no one to blame for my isolation."

"Except the Company."

"I didn't blame them because I was brainwashed to believe that the monotony and isolation of my life was for the good of All...until I felt the clean air Below."

With a pinch of Katya's tea in the bottom of their mugs, they poured on hot water, sniffing the oily green perfume as they talked.

"Hours standing in that hot suit night after night was for nothing! Once I knew the air was safe to breathe, I had to see if there was a way out."

Aaron put his arm around her shoulders and hugged her close. "And I saw your rag markers when I was on duty."

"How did you find them? Why did you walk down the tunnel?"

Aaron laughed. "I was bored and angry! You know I was helping others leave the Dome and I kept bumping into my father. Your guard partner became erratic and father insisted I take his place to make sure you weren't sick too."

"Paul wasn't sick," said Candy, "and I hope he's safe. Paul was simple not sick. Because our job was simple, Paul seemed the ideal guard but he had no idea about breaking rules or obeying orders. He did as he was told, standing at a door for twelve hours but had no room in his head to comprehend much else."

"I'm sorry," said Aaron, pulling her to him, "I wish I could give you news of him."

"So you walked down the tunnel..."

The Standing Stone – The Gathering

"...And found your markers. The message in the dirt was a warning. I didn't want you heading off into trouble if I could help you another way."

"How far did you get?"

"Not far. I was always running back for the Comfort break in case the alarm went off."

"So you didn't see the standing stone?"

"No but you think they're special?"

"Very," said Candy, "They're made of rock from the beginning of the earth, maybe from the beginning of time. Think of the stories they could tell if we only knew how to ask."

The following morning Candy rose with the sun and went into the back field and called the sheep. Fluff and Clouds' mother Mellow finished weaning them a month ago but seemed still full of milk and Hetty and Betty were always patient as long as they could be together. Candy talked to her sheep. By the time Aaron found her, she had four buckets of sheep's milk in the dairy.

"Doesn't look much like a dairy," said Aaron, standing in the doorway of the derelict barn.

"It faces north, has a door at either end to allow even more cool air in and, once I've covered these and found a place for them to stand, I'll fix that bit of roof. Once that's done, I'll clean down. The floor is stone and will be easy to keep clean," said Candy, covering her buckets with clean rag and tying them with string.

"So you're making...?"

"Butter and maybe cheese."

"But you can't take them to the Trading."

Candy, her face covered in dirt and her hair straggling behind her ears, looked up from the buckets.

"Sorry, no, okay but how are you going to get them to the Trading?"

"I'm not, but I am hoping to transport some to Katya. Maybe there are ways to get samples there, certainly of cheese and then I can take orders."

"You know how to make cheese?"

Candy couldn't restrain the slight smile that quirked from her lips. "Kind of. Look, I know the principles and I'll have to use the resources at hand along the way."

"Okay, so where are you going to get a butter churn?"

Candy's face lit up this time and she grabbed his hand. "Come on, Doubting Whisperer, I'll show you."

The second barn was inaccessible by the front door but Candy climbed through a gap in the side wall and Aaron followed. The end of the barn was gloomy as the roof was in tact but gradually, brown dusty shapes appeared in the murk. Candy squeezed into a corner and beckoned Aaron over.

"Will you help me?"

Together they lifted and pulled the wooden churn from its shelter into the open air like treasure from a Pharaoh's tomb. Aaron found a long piece of oak in the barn and they shored up the stone work in the side wall with a make shift lintel before dusting off Candy's machine.

"It really is only dirty," said Aaron, examining the lid and fitting it to the drum.

The Standing Stone – The Gathering

"And there's so much more in there! I can't wait to show you my idea for working in the evenings!"

The division between the tribes occupied Fern's mind as she moistened Nia's brow and lifted her head, trying to persuade water into her mouth. Nia either lay still as death or thrashed her head, calling out strange words in a gargling tongue. After each of these episodes, Fern held back her tears and settled Nia with gentle words and tender touches. Into the early hours of the morning, Fern held her vigil, arguing with herself at her own selfishness. She longed for Nia to be well, Nia who had taken the place of her mother and loved and guided her so well but she also needed Nia to help her rectify the dissent among the tribes. She worried that her prayers for Nia were awash with selfish intent and would, therefore, come to no good and yet, the goddess had always been with her so would she abandon her now?

As the light of the sun hallowed the day from behind the mountain and the birds woke the world with song, Fern's head began to nod at her task. With Nia sleeping gently and less hot than she was, Fern wrapped Nia's cloak about her body and stepped out into the summer's morning. She splashed her face with water and walked away from the huts to the river. Its song rose to greet her as she walked down to the beach and she marvelled at the boat, tied to the pier, bobbing in the water. It was icy cold on her toes but she stood for a moment, wriggling her feet and yawning. A peace fell over her as she took another step into the river. She held out her arms and shut her eyes, allowing her body to be filled with the diversity and power of nature. With a deep breath and a sigh, she made her way back to her house.

Nia lay awkwardly, trying to sip from a bowl of water.

"Nia!" cried Fern. Tears fell down her cheeks and she didn't try to stop them.

"Ah, there you are," said Nia, lying back.

"I was so worried! The storm, well it went on and on and I couldn't find you..."

"Hush, but you did and I thank you, child, with all my heart. My arm feels heavy but you have set it well."

"What happened?"

"I went for herbs and greens for the pot and found myself by the river. I found orache first and was picking that when I saw what I thought was marsh samphire. I had to climb out almost into the river and it wasn't samphire, of course. The last thing I remember is the rain hurting my eyes and then slipping into the mud."

"I went to the pool. Cerridwen showed me where you were."

"Bless the goddess," said Nia, squeezing Fern's arm. "But I see worry in your eyes even though I am better. What's happened Fern?"

Fern told Nia about the events in the Council hut before going to find Belle to pass on the news that Nia's fever had lifted but that she was not to be disturbed. Rowan and Bramble were still tucked up on one sleeping mat, snoring gently.

The Standing Stone – The Gathering

"Rowan's no bother," said Belle, "You've no need to worry about her. You look like you could do with some sleep though."

"And I will but Nia still needs me."

"Don't take all upon yourself, child," insisted Belle, "I'll get Aled to make sure you've wood for a few days and you go and get some sleep."

"I'll make food for Nia and myself first, Belle, and listen to any advice she may have. Then I will sleep."

Belle laughed, stopping her mouth and glancing at the girls but they did not stir. "You are your mother's daughter, Fern and may the goddess bless you."

Fern smiled, her eyes drooping as she accepted Belle's hug and two bowls of porridge.

Later that day, after both Fern and Nia had slept, Fern lay beside Nia as she spoke to her about the divisions in the village.

"We cannot fight them and we would be foolish to withdraw our help from tasks that benefit us all."

"But that's not fair!"

"Who says it has to be? Our ways are so because we believe that all have equal worth and deserve the same food, shelter, love and kindness as another but some only think of themselves."

"But then we will be working for nothing!"

"Doing what?"

"Well, clearing the field and...and building the new watering ground."

"They may have helped lift a few trees from the ground but little else. We will clear it and use our tame horses to plough. From what you say, Adalbern and Mara want nothing to do with it."

"You think?"

"I do, Fern. Neither Adalbern nor Mara's people are farmers. We are still learning while they remain hunting folk, dependent on others."

"I hate the idea we work for them."

"Now Fern, hate takes much energy in a detrimental way. Our tasks come first, of course and if they don't want to live in the Weaving House, then we shall weave in it! With new sheep coming in, we will have plenty of fleece!"

"But it was Adalbern's dagger that was to buy the sheep."

"It was a promise."

"With Mara whispering in his ear, I doubt he'll keep it."

"I am surprised by her," said Nia, shaking her head. "She seemed happy with our ways when she first moved here. You must watch her closely."

"Lugh is helping us with the watering ground," said Fern, "He feels abandoned by his sister."

"She states she works for her villagers best interests but I see a woman with selfish motives."

"So how do we pay for new sheep if Adalbern retracts his offer?"

"Ask the goddess, Fern. If it is to be, she will provide. Now, leave me to rest. Go find your young man or something and in the morning, I shall be back to normal."

The Standing Stone – The Gathering

The following day, Nia was a little better but was still too weak to stand for more than a few moments while she took a few steps.

"I'll be better with more rest," she insisted, "I've not missed a Gathering since you were born!"

As Fern's village assembled their goods together for the Gathering, murmurs of discontent ran round the cooking fires. Hours had been spent making baskets which the Tall Folk now filled with their cloth and clothes while Fern's village had a few meagre baskets of gloves and mittens. Many of the women had worked together, weaving the cloth but it seemed the Tall Folk were to get the benefit. Fern tried to reassure them as she walked from fire to fire, that the goddess knew of their efforts and that they would be recompensed. There was a sadness among the women as many of them had called the Tall Women friend and had believed them to be.

Fern's feet began to walk to the mound and she let them until her mind decried that the river bank for the new watering ground was to be her destination. Much of the scrub had been cleared from the bank, allowing tiers of clay to be fashioned, banked and supported by stone. Two A-frames stood to the side, her design already aiding with constructing the basins before they would be used again to move the water.

Fern walked to the furthest edge of the excavations before descending to the river, using the remnants of foliage to help her. The river was quiet here, lapping around two big stones in the centre of the water as it carried on downstream. As the water was low near the shore, Fern waded out to her thighs and clambered on top of the first large boulder, luxuriating in the warmth of the sun drenched stone. She lay on her back as the sun rose above her, the cry of a buzzard alerting her. She shielded her eyes as the massive bird came into view, circling in leisurely curves as another bird flew to join it. As the birds disappeared into the distance, Fern turned onto her stomach and leaned over the edge of the stone. Closer to the water at this edge, she saw fish darting from her shadow and the movement of tiny stones, shifted by the current. As one large stone rolled away, she glimpsed something glistening in the water.

Her arm would not reach so with some trepidation, Fern lowered herself into the river beside the shining object and found herself up to her neck in water. She wanted to use her feet as fingers to locate it but was scared to disturb the river bed and cover up her prize. The only thing to do was to dive but as she could not swim, this was a challenge. She tied back her hair with a band of rag and another on the end of her plait before trying two dips below the water, holding her nose and closing her eyes.

As she took a deep breath, she saw a shimmer by a small rock, just as she had seen it before so, pinching her nostrils together and with her eyes wide open, Fern dived down to the rock and retrieved the shiny treasure. Once back on the bank, she tucked the heavy object into the band of her trousers and set off back up to the village, as the voices of men could be heard, making their way to continue working on the boat and watering ground.

Chapter 10

Rachel spent a happy week finishing her bunting and weeding her raised beds. Oliver stopped by daily and seemed genuinely interested in the Midsummer fayre.

"The house is starting to feel like my home," he said, sipping tea at the kitchen table, "The office is wired in and my bedroom furniture is being delivered tomorrow."

"You seem happier."

"Oh, I am. Sorry I've been such a grump. Once the new TV is installed, you'll have to come round for a movie night."

"You're not converting the barn now?"

"I will but I'm looking forward to a couple of months without builders and electricians around. A bit of peace to work on building up my client list and getting my house how I want it and I'll be back to normal."

Rhys was absent until the next Saturday when he arrived on his bike, soaked to the skin by a sudden downpour.

"Now the baby's sleeping better, Mr Evans doesn't need me," he explained as he sat in Rachel's lounge in his boxer shorts and a blanket. "And Huw at the farm is using the Land Rover more now, so I've been looking for work I can reach by bus or bike."

"Any luck?"

"Not yet but did you know Euros Jones is selling the stud on the way to Llanybydder?"

"Don't think I know him," admitted Rachel as another cloud burst on the cottage, rattling the windows.

They sat in comfortable silence until the rain eased.

"That farm's been in their family for almost two hundred years but his son is into cars and women, from what I've heard, and his daughters have young children so he and Helen have been working pretty much alone these past five years."

"And it's all become too much?"

Rhys nodded. "Euros had a pacemaker fitted last month and they made the decision then. I spoke to Helen in the shop, to see if I could help but they can't afford to pay anyone. Horses cost more than they bring in unless you've a balanced, expansive breeding programme and, preferably, a waiting buyer."

"Now I think of it," said Rachel, "I have met Helen. She collected Mrs Davies after her perm at the shop. I might have misheard but doesn't she look after donkeys as well?"

"Yeah and old horses and goats. It's more like a sanctuary up there than a thriving stud!"

"Will they move far?"

"Helen has her eye on a modern bungalow on the edge of Llanllwni with a back garden and an option to buy an acre at the end of it but her main concern is the animals."

"Won't they sell the farm with the stock?"

"Yes, yes but who's going to want the other old, sick animals?"

Rachel loaded the burner with more logs as rain doused the house.

"Let's hope Mother Nature gets this load out of her system before next weekend," said Rhys, as the noise abated, "By the way, Beth has signed me up for a stall."

"Great, which one?"

Rhys turned to her as she sat on the sofa beside him and took her hand. "I want to tell you something first."

Rachel shivered but Rhys squeezed her hand.

"It's not bad or anything, don't worry, just awkward for a shy geek to put into words."

Rachel smiled, her shoulders relaxing as she placed her hand on Rhys' arm.

"I love you, Rachel. I love being here and the land and the mound and you but I'm gay."

"I know."

Rachel chuckled at Rhys' shocked face.

"But...how?"

"The picnic. You were trying to be different."

"Ah, right. I should have expected you to see through that one. I'm sorry but I wanted to be sure about what I was feeling. I care about you and I wanted to spoil you."

"I know and I loved it."

"But you kissed me back."

"And it was like kissing the kindest and best of mates," said Rachel, hugging him as he put his arm around her.

"Thank goodness," he said, kissing the top of her head, "I've been so worried and I couldn't get here."

"I did wonder if your attention was a ploy to put Oliver off."

"It did cross my mind, I'll admit but you don't believe all his new charitable malarkey, do you?"

"He's just making amends."

Rhys sat back from her, his eyes shining in a serious face. "Please be careful. There's something lurking beneath that squeaky clean exterior."

"He just wants to be friends, stop worrying. He's new too and it's not easy meeting people."

Rhys shook his head. "You're too trusting, too kind."

"Maybe but I was surrounded by secrets and lies throughout my childhood, playing 'happy families' while my parents had affairs. Oliver is Beth's brother, remember, so he can't be all bad. He made a mistake, a big one, I'll grant you and now he's living with the consequences. He met me, made a total idiot of himself and now wants to make amends and start again. I'd be a wicked person not to give him a chance."

"Just don't put yourself in danger, that's all. Let people know where you are."

"I will, I promise so, what stall are you running next week?"

Rhys hung his head before looking at her sideways with a grin. "I'm in the stocks for the kids to throw wet sponges at me."

Aaron was right. There was no time to make butter or cheese before the Trading. He had set off the comm so his father's team could trace them. Candy continued the pretence of making butter and cheese while she planned her next move. She showed him the loom in the barn and the remnants of a frame to twist and weave wool that stood on the floor like a ghostly harp.

"I'll need to wash the wool in the river before I can make a start on anything," she told him as they dusted off the machines and took them into the cottage.

She saw Aaron's eye flick to the corner cupboard of the dresser where he'd hidden the comm before alighting on the bed they were moving.

"Then there's carding and spinning. It will all take a while but it's another skill I can practise which will benefit me for next year. Stay Aaron. Stay and learn the skills to survive here. Wood work is useful, building with stone too and hedge laying."

Aaron hung his head as his grey blue eyes misted. "I can't."

Certain he was sleeping soundly, Candy left her bed in the barn and went into the cottage with her lantern. Retrieving the two packs and a special treasure she had hidden in the blanket box, she made her way to the stable. Whispering softly to Afon, Candy circled the barn, leading him down to the river and across to the other side. She turned only once to look back at the home she was leaving behind.

With her lantern hanging on the end of her staff, Candy led Afon along the riverbank. They made diversions, heading inshore as the river twisted or dropped in steep falls but they always returned to the

The Standing Stone – The Gathering

water. It was difficult to judge how far she travelled and she hoped the morning light would still reveal the range of hills she would need to climb to find her way to Katya.

She trudged on, ignoring the tears that coursed her cheeks and the heartache she carried in her chest. She had wanted to believe Aaron cared for her, even after overhearing his conversation in the woods but he had betrayed her to his father. He didn't care. It was all an act. She'd even dared to dream that he loved her and they would defy his father and set up home together. She scolded herself that the yearning she felt for him was a childish crush, building him up to be her saviour and worshipping him as one and maybe it was but he was the first man she had spent time alone with whom she could see herself loving and the pain in her heart did not abate.

Through the night they walked beneath a cloudless sky, swollen with the weight of planets and stars. Though struggling beneath her burden of sadness, Candy was lifted by the bright lights above her, comforted by Inanna's girdle embracing her. When a suitable hollow in the bank emerged, she tied Afon's lead rope to a rock, pulled out a blanket and curled up, exhausted and slept.

Afon woke her to the dawn chorus and a bright chilly morning. Over the river, in the distance, were the hills she had hoped to see. She reached into her pack for her treasure.

Though the back of the mirror was crafted in metal, it weighed fairy light in her hand and her fingers lingered on the exquisite twists of ivy and flowers, fashioned with delicate care across its back. The glass was fresh and clear, protected as it was by a soft cloth stuffed with sheep's wool. She held it in front of her.

Unlike her watery reflection, dark circles of weariness and sadness were her eyes and red lines of salt scoured her cheeks. Dipping in the water, she washed her face, the cool clear water waking her to a new day. She propped the mirror in the hollow and took the comb from her pack. With Afon nuzzling the grass beside her, she teased out her hair and let it fall to her shoulders, rose red in the early morning light. She smiled. She didn't need Aaron or any man to make her life. She had everything she wanted. She had neighbours and Katya was her friend. No one placed boundaries or restrictions on her. She would come back from the Trading and live with Afon and her sheep.

With a lighter heart, she led Afon downstream to a suitable crossing point and climbing onto his back, Candy set off for the hills. She ate a piece of biscuit and chewed on dried meat until a wisp of smoke tickled her nose. Turning towards the smell, she saw a dwelling, partly hidden by trees and walked Afon towards it.

The stone wall around the homestead was in good repair and the barn behind it had a sound roof. As she neared the gate, a grey haired man with tufty eye brows appeared through the doorway of the cottage, pointing a shot gun towards her.

"Please!" called Candy, "I mean no harm! May we rest a moment and ask directions to 'The Valley of the Horse'?"

The Standing Stone – The Gathering

The man lowered the gun a little. "Are you sick?"

Candy shook her head.

"Where you come from?"

Candy pointed up stream.

"The Jackson's place?"

"I don't know." She grabbed Afon's mane as weariness took over her. "I buried the man lying on the bed. He had been dead a while."

A small round face appeared under the arm of the man, quickly followed by a round body which hurried towards her. "Put down that gun at once, Bill Turner! Can't you see she's fit to drop?"

Candy slide from Afon's back, into the arms of the woman.

"I'm Alice, dear and this is my old man, Bill. He'll see to your horse."

"Afon," whispered Candy.

"Bill will see to Afon and I'll make you some warm milk with a touch of cinnamon and honey, don't you think?"

Candy nodded, content to be led into a warm room that was kitchen and living room and to forget, just for a moment, her painful past and uncertain future. Cradled by the Welsh blanket in the armchair by the fire, she smelled cakes on the griddle, making her mouth water. She wriggled her toes as the warmth of the welcome rekindled her spirits.

"Thank you," said Candy, taking her milk. "I hadn't realised how tired I was."

"Cakes won't be long and then you can have a rest. We'll not disturb you. We've plenty to do outside."

"You're very kind, thank you."

"That's the way of folk around here," insisted Alice, "Two, no three autumn's ago, Bill stayed up at Brian Mann's farm a full ten days, helping with the farm and getting wood chopped when Brian fell and broke his leg and Bill weren't the only one. Then last spring, when the weather turned cold, Brian alone saved twenty of our sheep and lambs from the snow while two other neighbours helped patch the roof of the big barn to house them. Brian brought us extra feed too, at no cost to us..."

Candy's eyes closed to the gentle chatter as the warm milk relaxed her body. Strong arms lifted her from her chair and she stirred a little but as she snuggled beneath the woollen blankets, she soon fell back to sleep.

Alone, except for the sleeping form of Nia, Fern examined her find from the river by the light from the fire. The misshapen lump could be mistaken for the mess left behind from metal work, that Fern had seen by Adalbern's kiln, except that it glowed golden orange. It was so big that she couldn't contain it in her palm without it being seen. She knew it would be enough to buy sheep, probably more and weighed twenty times more than Mara's gold ring.

She showed her treasure to Nia when she awoke.

The Standing Stone – The Gathering

"We are truly blessed by the goddess, Fern. That nugget is worth a great deal. You must seek out the Weighmaster at the Gathering."

"No, you do it. He'll think me a child and not pay me enough and..."

"I'm not going to the Gathering," interrupted Nia.

"But you must!"

"Fern, you must lead the village to the Gathering."

"I can't! I don't know the way and I certainly can't ride a horse!"

"But you must and you do know the way. Adalwin will be with you. He will help you, as will Aled and Celyn."

"Oh, Nia!"

Fern buried her face in Nia's neck, abandoning herself to the sobs that overwhelmed her. She cried for the unfairness of life, Nia's accident preventing her from travelling but more than that, she cried for the last semblance of her carefree childhood being ripped from her. The Gathering was a place of fun, of fire, jugglers, sword swallowers, exotic dancers and musicians. It was a magical place where the real world ended and the faery magic of childhood stories wrapped you in its spell. But instead of searching out trinkets, shells and feathers or dancing in the firelight she would be meeting traders and attempting to seal bargains for salt and tools, chickens and sheep.

"You can do this," said Nia, gently, "Your mother did it carrying you on her hip."

"But she had father."

"You have Adalwin."

"And our village?"

"They trust you, Fern, as do I."

Fern wiped her eyes and sat up. "Then tell me more of the Weighmaster and how I should deal with him."

"I shall and which traders to seek for all the village needs. We must also decide who is to stay behind."

"I know. Every year I dreaded being left behind while today, I would happily pass my burden to another and stay here."

"There will be time for you and Adalwin," said Nia, "and with Mara's seducing of his father, maybe you should jump the fire together."

Fern blushed. "How do I know it is his wish?"

Nia sighed. "It is many years since a man looked at me as Adalwin does you but you feel it, don't you?"

Fern's feet carried her to the mound, sunlight shimmering through the fresh young leaves, a pastel carpet at her feet. Climbing down to the sacred pool, she knew what she must do.

The woman who looked up from the reflective water had dark eyes, like her own but her hair was lighter and finer, a halo of copper wire framing her head. Full red lips hinted at a smile and Fern closed her eyes, her heart beating in her ears. A gentle voice spoke but there was strength behind the words and Fern listened as her mother passed to her the wisdom of ages.

The magic of her line fizzed in her veins and when she opened her eyes, a proud young woman with rich dark hair looked back at her. She lifted her chin and felt something beneath her fingers on the ground. She tied the leather head band, with its centre piece of moonstone, around her forehead. She was a warrior with the heart of a goddess.

Chapter 11

With just two days to go before the fund raising Midsummer fayre, the grounds of the University were awash with people, erecting the main marquee and knocking in signs to show stallholders where to place their stands. Some stalls were under cover and these were erected as the bleep of reversing lights brought vans loaded with equipment, including Rhys' stocks. There was to be a rota for his stall but Rachel hoped to leave the Lucky Dip at some point and capture his ordeal on film.

She stood at the bottom of a step ladder, passing up bunting which Oliver fixed to the railings. He was dressed in full camouflage gear, the irony of which was that as no one else was over dressed in such a way, he stood out like a flamingo at a penguin party.

She tried not to look at him as it made her giggle but instead, watched the fayre growing like a small village, and thought instead of Lucy's impending visit. With Rhys' help, the spare bedroom was ready, fresh curtains at the windows and sweet smelling cotton on the bed. She'd been into town herself to buy groceries and wine, surprised how hard it was to choose for a friend she thought she knew. All was tidy in the cottage now the boxes were gone so she would have time to spend with Lucy as soon as she arrived.

While preparing for Lucy's visit, Rhiannon's words, that she should embrace the spirit of the horse, kept coming into her mind. Perhaps Lucy would have time to go for a ride, a happy reminder of their childhood that Rachel realised she missed.

A cry of 'Beer!' went up as two large crates were taken from the back of a van. Helpers dropped tools and made for the much needed refreshment.

"You coming for a beer?" she called up to Oliver.

"We've only to the gate to do," he said, coming down the ladder, "Shall we finish it?"

"Sure," she said, helping him move the steps.

By the time they reached the beer crates, a violin was playing a catchy tune and a dance had begun so they sat on the grass to watch. The evening sun shone above the hill as Rhys came over and pulled her up to join in. She gave her bottle to Oliver, laughed at his grumpy face, kicked off her sandals and allowed herself to be led into the circle. Siân was opposite her, trying to keep up with the rhythm, but they were both soon able to turn, spin and take their partner at the appropriate time.

In her vest top and cut down shorts with her hair loose, flowing behind her, Rachel was alive. At this time, at this moment, right now, she could feel it. For so long she had clung to the past, dwelling on details she could do nothing to change. Here, beneath the warm summer sun with her friends and neighbours, she was living right now. No thoughts filled her head. Only the uneven grass under her bare feet, the blue sky, the sunshine and the music compelling her to dance, occupied her senses. She cheered the violinist before floating back to Oliver.

He stood up as she approached, handing her the beer bottle. "You'd better drink up and help me finish the bunting."

Lucy arrived just after midday with a trunk full of luggage and a large bottle of champagne.

"I thought perhaps tomorrow night to crack this one," she said, waving it before finding a space in the fridge. "You expecting an army? There's enough food in here to feed one!"

Rachel laughed for the tenth time in as many minutes. In the same room as Lucy, it felt like no time had passed between them. The final bag was brought in and they were about to sit in the garden with coffee, bread and cheese.

"Can we get something out of the way first?"

"Sure," said Rachel, "You okay?"

"Come here," said Lucy, pulling Rachel into a proper hug. "I'm so sorry, Rach. All you went through with your parents and Jack... and then Marcus...I'm really glad to be here."

Rachel hugged her back, a lump rising in her throat. "Thanks, Luce, it's good to have you here but I'm starting to find ways to deal with the past. The fayre tomorrow, raising money to help other mums and babies is a start."

Lucy stepped back. "It's a wonderful idea, perfect to take your mind off your problems but it doesn't mean they're dealt with, my lovely."

"I know that," said Rachel, picking up the tray, "But I had to make a start somewhere."

"You weren't tempted to just give them a wadge of cash rather than work your bum off making bunting?"

Rachel laughed. "I've missed you, Luce. You won't believe how much."

They sat in front of the wood burner in the gifts they had bought for each other; Rachel in a fluffy penguin night shirt and Lucy in a sheep onesie.

"So that's why I've come to Wales, to start over."

"And Abigail?"

"She's saying she doesn't want to move and leave her friends but she's only six. I'm hoping to find a property while I'm here and then bring her once the school's break up."

"And you'll leave the house and business with Tristan?"

"Not a chance! Tristan doesn't know anything about horses! No, it's all being sold. I've a good solicitor and an even better barrister waiting in the wings if things get messy. But it shouldn't. Catching ones husband in the marital bed, on film I might add, gives one the upper hand somewhat!"

"Oh, Luce, that must have been awful!"

Lucy sipped her hot chocolate, her cheeks flushing pink. "I already had other concrete evidence, receipts, emails that kind of stuff and I handled it well at the time. Freaked out a bit a couple of days later but he was gone by then so I never showed him how much he hurt me."

"What an idiot!"

"Me or him?"

"Him of course!" laughed Rachel, "Trading his life for...how did you put it?"

"Plastic tits and the IQ of a stick of celery."

They both laughed.

"So you've viewings arranged?"

"Two tomorrow, late afternoon so I'll come to the fayre with you if that's okay?"

"Of course."

"And two on Sunday, then I'll be out of your hair."

"You're welcome to stay as long as you like."

"That's good of you, Rach but I'll not outstay my welcome. I'd love to bring Abby here though, later in the summer."

"Be lovely to meet her."

"Sure?"

"Yes, sure. I'll never forget Jack but I can't keep away from children forever. Hey, I nearly forgot, I know you're viewing properties with land but is the horse stud just outside Llanybydder on your list?"

"The one with more sick animals than fine horses?"

"That'll be the one only, if you do consider buying it, I have an idea."

While she ate a chunk of home-made bread, liberally spread with butter, and a bowl of chicken soup, Candy answered Bill's questions and told him and Alice how she came to be living at the Jackson's farm.

"We've not heard of any Dome, love but Katya's story about the religious cult definitely rings a bell," said Alice, "But we're not originally from this part of the country."

She sat on the chair opposite Candy and picked up her wool and crochet hook as she talked. "We'd seen the news on the television, governments arguing about who was investing money in overseas weapons, denying supporting terrorist organisations and secret films of bomb factories and nuclear missiles, but had no idea that it would all come to a head so soon."

"We were young then, duck, only in our twenties and we didn't take much notice of such things."

"You're right there, Bill. Anyway, we tried for a baby and after getting the news that it was probable I couldn't conceive, we decided to take a fortnight break in a cottage in Wales."

"And here we are, more than forty years later."

"So this isn't your house?"

Bill laughed. "It is now! We rented it, paid half up front, arrived here and the world changed. We didn't find out details until we went into town. They had a radio working there for a couple of years after the explosion but there's no communication any more."

"And your families? Could you find out if they were safe?"

"I was brought up in a children's home and Bill was brought up by his grandma. She died a few years before we came here. We didn't look back, Candy. The enormity of what had happened to the world shocked us, and many other survivors, for many months but people pulled together and we all look forward now."

"Is the town where the Trading is?"

Alice smiled. "No, love, two different places. The Trading is a meeting for those from all over the country while the town is for local people. There are a few shops but the weekly market is the busiest time where we can barter and meet other neighbours."

"Is it close? Is it nearer than the Trading?"

"It's probably the same distance," said Bill, "But only takes a day as the walk is a flat one."

Candy's head buzzed with information. She had thought Katya her nearest neighbour but Bill and Alice were even closer and there was a town only a day from them.

"So you can show me the way to 'The Valley of the Horse'?"

"We know the place," said Bill, clearing the bowls from the table, "but if it's the Trading you want, it's out of your way to go there. We're going to the Trading. Come with us and meet your friend, Katya there."

"When will you leave?"

"A week, maybe ten days."

"What if Aaron comes looking for me?"

"Will he?"

"He may come this way but I suppose he might go straight to Katya's house. I hope there won't be trouble because of me."

"Folk around here can take care of themselves," said Bill. "I for one don't like a greeting that includes a twelve bore but until we are sure of people, we keep them away. This community operates on trust and kindness. We don't need greedy or selfish people here."

"That sounds a little uncharitable, love and we do welcome people, and help them, if they want to fit in but there were bad times four summers back when it didn't rain. Two young men had moved into Wym Jones' farm when he died and had messed about with the river on their land."

"Wells were drying up," continued Bill, "and those two greedy sods tried to hold water on their land and force the locals to pay for it before they would release it. They posed and threatened while water was rationed for people and animals, until the town acted together and they were driven from their land."

"Not neighbourly, not nice, is what I felt at the time," said Alice, "but you can't let others control you like that, not with blackmail."

"I can see that," said Candy. She sat looking at her lap.

Alice rose from her chair, laying down her crocheted shawl. She put her hand on Candy's shoulder. "So you'll be wanting to know our routine, then?"

"Sorry?"

"So you can help out before we ride to the Trading, if you want to stay, of course."

The day before the Gathering was warm but humid and the three tribes sweated as they organised their wares. Agnes had secreted cloth to Fern's village for them to sell, a decision made by all the Tall Folk women, for which Fern was very grateful. Not only did it give them more bartering power but, more importantly, it proved the friendships they had made with the Tall Folk women were genuine. Fern's village decided, at Council, who stayed and who went. A mixture of joy and disappointment hung over the people but they trusted all decisions made.

As the sun rose the next day, with hugs and promises to bring back gifts for those who remained behind, men, women and children, led by Fern and Adalwin, headed for the hills on their long journey to the Gathering. There was no movement from Adalbern's village.

"They sleep long because they drink much," said Adalwin, walking beside Fern. "It is best to leave early so small legs don't have to run."

Fern laughed. She had expressed a wish at Council to lead her people on foot while the horse she would have ridden, shared the carrying of their goods and would be helpful when they brought back more sheep. She had suppressed worries about Adalbern's promise to buy new livestock by assuring the villagers that the goddess would provide but she told no one, not even Adalwin, of the gold nugget that nestled in the bottom of the leather pouch she carried across her body. Her food for the day sat on the top and she smiled to herself at the thought of presenting the gold to the Weighmaster covered in sheep's cheese.

They traversed two hills and as they reached the top of a third, Fern stood and turned about, checking the countryside around her. Descending this hill was a steep climb but at the bottom, on a track through a forest, they would be on the way to the crossing and she hoped they could make camp on the other side.

Though none of the Olds travelled with them, they made slow progress down the steep hill, laden as they were with baskets. Fern's village owned only six horses and two had been left behind so much of their produce had to be carried, as well as food, water and shelter for the journey. As they reached the bottom of the valley, the sun was at its zenith and all were glad to walk into the relative cool shade of the forest path.

They stopped on the road at the sound of water and walked the horses to a stream to drink before quenching their own thirst and sharing out food. They walked on, through the tall, broad trees along a track no wider than two horses as the afternoon grew cooler as the sun dropped behind the hill.

They heard the river before they saw it, like the rumble of distant thunder. Tired legs moved faster and small children were coaxed harder to reach the crossing where they would have a chance to rest. The trees became sparser, tree trunks visible between those still standing until the trees finally ran out and the track opened out onto a large oval beach of mud and stones. The children squealed at the sight of the river while Fern was disappointed to see only one raft tied to the jetty with two men standing by it. She and Adalwin approached them as parents tried to keep their children from the water.

"Good day," said Fern, making a small sharp nod of a bow to the men as she approached.

"Good day," they answered in the same manner.

"We seek a crossing on the river. What will be the tally?"

"We are not for hire," said the younger of the men. His black greasy hair stuck to his head and one eye wandered to look at his nose.

"Why say you this?" asked Fern. "We have come to cross for the Gathering as we have always done."

"Not this time," smirked the young ferryman, "You're not going anywhere."

Adalwin went to step forward but Fern stopped him.

"What say you?" she asked the other man.

The old ferryman peered at her through sad misty eyes. "I see less well every day," he said, "but you sound like young Fern."

"It is Fern."

"Then where is Nia?"

"She fell and hurt herself a week back. She is mending but is not well enough to travel."

"I am sorry to hear that," said the old man, "May the goddess bless her. I'm sorry, Fern. We have been paid to wait for another tribe. They will arrive before nightfall and we must take them across the river."

"If we went now, we could be over and you could get back."

"We cannot chance it," said the old man, shaking his head.

"We'll not get the rest of our payment if we're not here when they arrive."

"Mara," said Adalwin, under his breath.

"It was a woman who hired you?"

"Yes, a painted woman."

"She will pay those who serve her well," said the young man, "While you have nothing we want."

As Fern held Adalwin back again, a commotion broke out behind her. Riders had galloped into her tribe, disturbing their horses who charged off in different directions. Two ran for the water before spotting their mistake and as they pulled up, packages bouncing on their flanks, she saw two precious baskets fall into the water. The other horses galloped along the beach, men chasing them until they too pulled up, baskets and bundles falling onto the stones.

Mara, Adalbern and his entourage laughed at the disappearing horses before riding over to the ferrymen.

"It's our crossing," said Mara, "We pay these men."

"So I see," said Fern, "We will wait for you to cross and then follow after."

"Not if we don't send the ferry back," said Mara, circling her horse around Fern.

"Why would you do that?"

"We will arrive at the Gathering first and make the best deals," said Adalbern. "They write songs about Yellow Beard and have great respect for me."

"Then what difference does our arrival make to you?"

"None," said Adalbern, dismissing her with his hand. "Son, take one of the spare horses and come with me."

"No," said Adalwin, "I accompany Fern to the Gathering."

Adalbern spoke more words Fern did not understand and she looked around for Geirr but couldn't see him. Adalwin replied but Fern could not follow the conversation. Adalbern rode away with Mara close behind him, turning and grinning her wide mouthed smiled. Adalwin stood red faced next to Fern.

"She is taking my father from me," growled Adalwin.

"What?"

"He said to follow him or he would...no longer call me son."

"No!"

"She will bear him a son. Then Adalhard and I will be nothing."

"Is Adalhard here?" She turned looking for Adalwin's older brother but she could not see him and there was no sign of Geirr either. "You must go, Adalwin, with your father. You cannot let her take your birthright from you."

"I am not to lead the tribe, Adalhard is the elder. I will not go with my father."

"What will you do?"

"I will leap the fire with you."

It was late the following morning before the ferry returned across the river. When their horses had been startled, all the carefully wrapped eggs had been broken and other perishable goods crushed. Some of the villagers wanted to turn back as Adalwin and Fern

The Standing Stone – The Gathering

walked among them, helping to repack and setting up skins for shelter for the night. They were assured all would be well even though Fern worried that the ferry would not come back at all.

Only the old ferryman was visible as he pulled over onto the jetty, his hands slipping on the wet ropes. He stumbled as the raft bumped against the planking. Adalwin leapt on board to help him. As the villagers and horses stepped on board and the large raft rocked and creaked, Adalwin jumped back on the jetty and ran to Fern.

"He came but it is not allowed," he said, "There may be trouble on the other side."

"I will speak to the men," said Fern.

When she stepped on board, she thanked the old ferryman. He shook his head.

"Nia has always been kind to us," he said. "I remember the night that boy was born," he added, nodding his head to the far bank, "It were Nia that saved his and my wife's lives that night but he does not remember. I could not let you miss the Gathering so I came in Nia's name and my wife's memory."

"I will tell Nia of your kindness and bravery," said Fern, taking his hands. The moonstone in the band across her forehead began to pulse. The old ferryman's eyes opened wide as he peered at her. "By the goddess, it is Seren!"

He dropped her hands and turned away to his ropes, leaving Fern confused but with children and animals to supervise, she soon forgot the strange words of the ferryman.

As Adalwin helped the old ferryman secure the raft at the jetty on the other side of the river, they heard his son before they saw him.

"You stupid fool! You stupid ignorant old fool! She'll not give us our gold now and all because of you!"

With his hands secure behind his back and tied on his side to the bed, the young man was angry and the house stunk of his bodily functions as Adalwin, Fern and the ferryman entered.

"No, don't untie him yet," said the older man. "I will talk and he will listen. Don't worry, you get going or you'll be chasing those horses again!"

"Thank you," said Fern, "I will tell Nia all that you have done for us."

It was easy to follow the track the riders had taken and soon their spirits rose as they reached the top of a hill upon which they could see all the land before them. In the distance was the Wide Water, gleaming like a fat silver snake and they set off towards it, Fern hoping that this crossing would be less perilous than the first.

The following two days passed uneventfully and on the third night, they sat around the fire, singing as Fern had promised they would cross the Wide Water the next day.

As Nia had bid her, she wore the fur cape as the villagers approached the crossing and just as Nia had said, the boat men welcomed them, asking nothing for their conveyance. Fern insisted they accept a package from Nia, explaining there were healing oils and herbs within and the four men bowed and took the parcel with reverence, wrapping it in a skin and taking it to the boat house.

Though the water looked calm and flat, it was windy on the raft which spanned three times the size of the first one. The horses skittered as they rode the rolling waves but the boat men whispered to them and they soon stood calm and still. As the shoreline behind them disappeared, Fern's stomach lurched and she kept her eyes from the deep blue drop beneath her. Instead she told stories to the children about the naughty baby rabbit who wouldn't sit still and the baby owl who was afraid of the dark. With crusts to chew, the children soon forgot where they were and as a new shore appeared on the horizon, most had drifted off to sleep.

Fern stood with Adalwin who passed her a drink from a water skin.

"Our journey time is a good one?"

"Yes," said Fern, "We'll arrive in time for the Gathering."

Chapter 12

After a sound and refreshing sleep, Rachel woke with her alarm and crawled to the tiny window at the end of the bed, taking her quilt with her. The sun was up, bathing the yard with golden yellow light. Swallows flew back and forth, using her drive like a corridor and confirming her belief that they were nesting in one of the barns. Slipping into her soft penguin nightshirt, Rachel crept downstairs and lit the burner. With a long day ahead, she decided that a bath before breakfast was a good idea and by the time Lucy emerged in her onesie, Rachel was fresh and clean and ready to scramble eggs for breakfast.

Rachel parked her car and she and Lucy grabbed a few bags and walked into the University grounds. Voices and laughter rose from the tents. With just two hours to go before the fayre was officially opened by the mayor of Lampeter, finishing touches were being added to the stalls and perishable goods were emerging from plastic boxes.

As the University clock approached 10.30am, the PA was tested and the mayor delivered his speech, praising the organisers and wishing them well with fund raising for the baby unit. Rachel heard little of it as her stall was already surrounded by children, eager to dip into the tubs, brimming with sawdust from the saw mill at the Long Wood.

Lucy kissed her cheek at one point and indicated the coffee behind her but she struggled to find time to take a sip. The sun beamed on their endeavours as the minutes ticked by and just after midday, Rachel's queue became a trickle as families covered the grounds eating picnics or food they had purchased on site. Rhys appeared, tousle haired and wearing damp shorts.

"Bought you a pastie," he said, handing her a wrapped parcel, "Can you take a break?"

"I can't leave here until the tubs are empty but I must be nearly there," she said, taking money from two young girls in front of her as well as the pastie.

"Sit on that chair and eat," ordered Rhys, "I'll take over for a bit."

So she sat in the sun, biting into the warm pastry, drooling at the peppery meat inside. Her belly growled after the first mouthful as she realised how hungry she was. She watched Rhys, relaxed as always, talking gently to the children and wished, not for the first time, that he wasn't gay.

"But then he wouldn't be Rhys," said a voice by her ear.

She spun round to find Beth grinning at her and leapt to her feet. "I was just having some lunch."

Beth laughed, her fine blond curls dancing around her head like a halo. "You're entitled to a break, no need to apologise. Next time we'll make sure we've enough helpers for two per stall. He is a natural with children, isn't he?"

"How did you read my mind?"

"Easy to do sometimes with friends. How are you doing on the tubs?"

"Nearly out. I was going to have a check when the queue finished."

"Well the sticker tombola is sold out and they're almost out of balls at the football shoot out. Another hour, the main raffle to draw and then we're done."

"That's great news," smiled Rachel.

"And your bunting looks wonderful. I've had comments about it, you know. We'll take it down carefully and store it somewhere dry."

"Really? I'm just glad my first attempt did the job."

"You're pretty talented with that machine of yours." Beth leaned closer. "Better than a lot of people who shout about their skills."

"I like the machine," admitted Rachel, "Maybe I'll keep sewing after this."

Once her tubs were down to a handful of gifts and the crowds began to disperse, they took away the hubbub of the fayre and she heard music rising from the entertainment tent. Similar to the jaunty tune she had heard on Thursday evening, she felt her toes tapping as she packed away. Rhys had called it Ceilidh.

With the tubs on the floor, she sat at the low table and began counting her money into the bags provided until she caught herself wondering if there were places to dance locally. She stopped and looked out at the scene around her. Only a few members of the public remained as the stall holders, still smiling, packed away to the sound of the violin. She saw Beth shaking hands with a man in a suit and laughing and to her right she saw Ffion with a baby sling on her front. The cry of a new born baby made her belly squirm as Mrs Evans rocked the pram and Mr Evans shook hands with the mayor and proudly introduced his wife and child. A squeal followed by laughter made her turn and there was Rhys pursuing Siân with a bucket of wet sponges, egged on by the crowd.

As she laughed at Siân a thought rose in her mind that she hadn't seen Oliver all day but then was gone. In the distance she spotted a head full of blond curls glinting in the sunlight, quickly followed by a tall leggy body, as Lucy strode through the crowd, oblivious to the heads turning in her direction.

These are my friends and this is my life, here in Wales. She felt tears rising and a lump gathering at her throat, not for those she saw before her but for those she could not see. She had no man's arm to lean on or to win her a coconut at the shy and she hadn't a little boy to buy a balloon for or treat to a ride on the pony but no amount of wishing could change that. She cuffed at her eyes. Instead she had a life full of kind neighbours and friends and the prospect of any future she chose for herself.

"How did it go?" asked Lucy, bending down to give her a hug.

"Really well," said Rachel. She packed the last of the bags into an ice cream tub labelled 'Lucky Dip' and stood up. "And you?"

Lucy's eyes were shining. "I may cancel tomorrow's appointments, Rachel. I think I've found my new home."

"Really?"

"Yeah so would you like to elaborate about your idea for Euros' farm?"

"Of course and you know what?"

"What's that?"

"You and the childhood memories I hold dear of us together may hold the key to a door opening in the next chapter of my life."

"Really? I've done nothing but I'm so happy for you," said Lucy, hugging Rachel tightly.

Rachel clung to Lucy, her face buried in her sweet smelling hair, and whispered a prayer of thanks. "Blessed, Rhiannon. I will embrace the spirit of the horse."

It was a two day ride to the Trading so they camped by woods overnight. Bill and Alice had a large tent and were happy for Candy to share with them.

"It's an old tent but with a few patches it's holding up well," said Bill, knocking in tent pegs, "When we arrived, there was a camping shop in the town."

"So you bought it, all those years ago?"

Alice laughed. "We did and camped down by the river and were eaten alive by midges!"

"So nothing new comes to the shops now?"

"Not the shops, no but sometimes we do get goods that are old but only just discovered," said Bill, straightening up. "There were those car parts that Alfie filled his truck with, remember?"

The Standing Stone – The Gathering

"I do," said Alice, "And Brian Mann helped get the forge firing so metal could be shaped to make new tools and hinges and brackets."

"Will we find tools at the Trading?"

"Some but they've travelled far and cost a lot more. Have you need of tools?"

Candy explained about the state of repair of her bill hook and garden fork.

"That's only the wooden handles gone," said Alice, "There's plenty of folk who can fix them."

"If you dry your tools and then use your sharpening stone before you put them away, they'll last even longer," said Bill.

"I've so much to learn," admitted Candy.

"And we'll help you, love," said Alice, "Now, anyone for chicken soup?"

The sun was turning the sky pink as they led the horses down the road, along the ridge to the Trading. Bill pointed to their left at the field covered in tents.

"We'll pitch the tent and enter the Trading on foot. You with us Candy?"

Candy had stopped Afon's progress and was standing looking at the scene below her, leaning on her staff. The milky crystal at its top glowed in the light of the setting sun. She had stood in crowds in the Dome, when it was time to descend Below but she had never seen such a host of colourful humanity in one place. The camp site was busy but the Trading on the hill top was heaving with people and she could hear music on the wind. She turned Afon to follow Bill and Alice.

The people and music had thrilled her at first but she began to doubt she would find Katya in such a throng. The pain in her chest worsened as she wished that Aaron were with her. Sharing this experience and seeking advice and provisions together was what she wanted and she cuffed hurriedly at her eyes to prevent the tears forming. Bereavement pulled at her heart for the future that might have been with Aaron and fear shuddered through her body at the thought of the scenario she might find when she returned home.

Candy helped erect the tent and laid her sleeping roll at one end. Alice gave her a brown metal disc that she assured her was necessary to give to the man on the gate where the horses were to be housed.

"He will feed and water them. They will be safe," said Alice.

Without Afon, Candy felt even more alone as they skirted the bottom of the hill to the beginning of the winding path and began the steep climb as the sun hit the horizon sending streaks of light across the hills around them. Higher they climbed, hugging the inner most track as laughing folk descended and a man followed them, lighting torches along the pathway. As they rounded the final bend before reaching the summit, Candy cried out and pointed. Below her, not far in the distance stood mammoth standing stones set in a white circle that glistened and shone in the fuchsia light and beyond it, leading into the distance, was an avenue lined with more immense boulders.

The Standing Stone – The Gathering

"It's a magical landscape here, love," said Bill, "The ancient people knew how to celebrate nature and show respect for the Land."

"I want to go down there," said Candy, "I have to see those stones."

"There's no rush, don't you worry," said Alice, "There'll be plenty of time for you to talk to the stones."

As they climbed onto the Trading ground, warm air and smoke filled their faces while laughter, chatter and music bombarded their ears. Stalls were still Trading and Candy's nose twitched at the smell of roasting meat. She held onto Alice's belt and she onto Bill's as he led them towards the fire and soon Candy was sitting on a straw bale, fat dripping off her chin as she ate the succulent pork.

Away from the food stalls, Bill and Alice walked her round the Trading, pointing out the different trades and sellers, where they would come to barter in the morning. The air was chill on the hilltop, smoke from the fire mixing with the breath of the people but above her head, Candy felt Inanna with her, as the star studded sky felt close enough to touch.

As they completed their circuit of the hilltop and prepared to return to the camp site, dancing began around the fire as two drums lifted their beat to the sky. While one resounded like a heart beat that Candy felt deep inside, the other rattled and trilled and men and women danced.

"Katya!" cried Candy.

A dark haired young woman turned, her brown eyes full of surprise and delight as she ran across and hugged Candy.

"I was so worried," she said, into Candy's neck, "We waited as long as we could. What happened?"

Candy introduced Katya to Bill and Alice and with Bill's home made wind up torch in her pocket so she could find her way back to the camp site, she bid Bill and Alice goodnight. She spent a happy hour telling Katya the story of the past weeks and how she came to be with her new travelling companions.

"So the pull for Aaron was too much," said Katya, "Such a shame."

"I know. I could see the torment on his face in the last days we had together. He hated lying to me."

"Bill and Alice seem kind."

"They've been more than kind and they've offered to help me get organised on the farm. I tried so hard to carry on, even with the knowledge that Aaron would betray me. I started making butter and was going to try cheese and I've found a weaving machine in the derelict barn."

"We'd be happy to trade for your goods, Candy and we too will help you all we can with plants and seeds, you know that."

"Thanks so much," said Candy, accepting another hug, "Knowing I've people around who care really helps but I don't know what I'm going to find when I get home. I'm worried for the sheep, though they survived on their own before I found the cottage so I can only hope for their safety and in that case, part of me wants to go home with you and live in your valley and hide from the team from the Dome. How feeble is that?"

"Not feeble at all considering where you've come from and no one would blame you but I know you love your cottage. You can't go back alone and though Bill and Alice are kind, they would be no match for a team of armed men. You can come back with me, help us out for a week or so, learning while you're with us and then we can accompany you home."

"I don't want to put any of you at risk," insisted Candy, "I was worried Aaron would lead them over the hills to you."

"No strangers have come so, don't worry and you're our neighbour now. We won't let you come to harm."

They sat watching the fire as the last of the dancers drifted away and the drumming stilled.

"I saw the stone circle and avenue as we neared the Trading," said Candy, "I have to get down there."

"They are beautiful," admitted Katya, "but tell me what draws you to them."

Heat rose in Candy's face as she spoke.

"The goddess, Katya. Ever since finding the standing stone down the passageway in the Dome, I've felt loved and guided by a presence so vast and wonderful, I can't put it into words. I crave her wisdom at a time where others try to take me from the path I have chosen for my life."

"Then we shall go tomorrow afternoon, together."

"And if anything happens to me, promise me you will seek her guidance, Katya."

Katya laughed. "Nothing's going to happen here!"

"Promise me you will though and that you will go to the farm and save my animals and tell Afon what has happened to me."

"If that's what you want."

"I do. The animals and land are my responsibility now. Bill and Alice will help you."

"Stop talking like you're going to die or something! You're making me scared!"

"Sorry but I can't help thinking how insistent Aaron was that I go back to the Dome and his father is determined that I return and I don't really know why but he's a man used to getting his own way."

They walked down the path around the hill, the burning torches lighting their way. They parted with a hug and a promise to meet the next day to visit the stones and be back on the hill for the Midsummer Celebration. Candy wound her torch and was surprised how bright the light was that lit her feet. Head down she set off to find her tent, already looking forward to spending the following day with Katya among the standing stones.

Few lights showed on the camping ground as Candy picked her way through the guy ropes in search of Alice and Bill's tent. The ancient bivouac should have been easy to spot but many of the tents were recycled, old tents patched with new fabric. She found it at last and gently ran the zip up the opening, keeping her torch low to the ground as she crawled inside. Flipping onto her bottom to remove her boots, a chance glance to her left revealed Alice and Bill's sleeping compartment flapping open and no sign of her companions inside.

As her heart pounded in her chest, she sought excuses for Alice and Bill's absence. Perhaps they were catching up with friends or checking on the horses. Candy wound up the torch and shone it into the sleeping compartment revealing sleeping bags and bedding strewn over the floor.

She stood outside the tent and began counting her beats, desperate to slow her heart so she could think clearly. There was no reason for Aaron's father to take Alice and Bill, or none she could see. Deciding to check on Afon, her precious horse, given to her by her friend Katya, she walked towards his field but before she'd walked twenty paces strong arms gripped her torso from behind and a cloth was forced over her mouth. The last thought she had before drifting into unconsciousness, was an image of Katya, arms aloft in the circle of standing stones below the Trading.

Two days they walked through a wet, boggy landscape. Though she and Adalwin had told everyone to stick to the path, they were twice delayed as children wandered off and found themselves stuck. The second incident required a chain of men linking arms while Adalwin crawled along the thick branch they held, to rescue a boy. He was pulled from the stinking mud pool just before his shoulders were sucked under. After that, they made swifter, silent progress.

As they rose on the third day, the sun was already warm, burning away the clouds. They had finished their journey the previous day with firmer ground beneath their feet and the morning revealed the hilltop for the Gathering in the distance, a shining green mound with people already moving up to its summit.

Spirits were high as they packed away the willow branches and skins that made their make shift camp and lifted their precious goods onto the horses. With Fern and Adalwin leading the way, the tribe walked to the Gathering.

As they approached the field beneath the hill in which they would make camp, people sat around fires making breakfast and they were greeted and welcomed to the midsummer Gathering. Excitement and trepidation coursed through Fern's veins as she explained to those who asked that Nia was not with them. News spread quickly that Nia was unwell but soon Fern had a queue of people at her animal skin tent, asking for advice and healing. She sat cross legged on the grass with Nia's cloak around her and the herb bag in her lap. She was paid with food, beads, shells and pelts while her tribe fed her porridge, waiting patiently for her to lead them to the Gathering, just as Nia had always done. More people began to crowd her until Adalwin stood before them, his big blond face wearing a frown as he raised his arms.

"Stand back!" he cried, "Fern is tiring and needs to lead her people."

The Standing Stone – The Gathering

Most backed away but some people muttered, scowling at Adalwin and tried to push forward.

"This woman is the last to be healed today!" cried Adalwin. "You will leave!"

The people became rowdy and shouts broke out.

Fern let go of the woman's hand she held and stood up. "Lift me, Adalwin."

On Adalwin's shoulder, Fern addressed the crowd.

"Please forgive me, people of my land. I am not Nia but her student and I tire more easily than she. Adalwin is right, I must lead my tribe to the Gathering and be seen upon the hilltop but tomorrow, after I have walked my path around the stones and along the avenue, I will return. There will be time for healing then."

As she spoke, a great beam of sunlight descended from the sky, illuminating Fern and Adalwin, she, dark haired and swarthy skinned and he, golden haired and fair. The crowd gasped and bowed, some shuffling backwards, while others fell to their knees before her. The woman she had been healing stood up, ushering people back before taking Fern's hand as Adalwin lifted Fern to the ground.

"You have the knowing, young one," said the woman, whose bloodshot red eyes were clearing to white, "You are more powerful than you know. My sight is returning and the pain in my head is easing by your hand. I shall thank the goddess every day for sending you to me."

The woman pressed something into Fern's hand before walking away between the tents. Fern looked down at the tiny but heavy object that sat in her palm

171

and felt her heart quicken at the precious metal, sculptured into an owl.

Fern wore Nia's fur cape as she led her tribe to the Gathering. Head's turned to the diminutive woman beside the tall blond man and many, recognising the cape, bowed to her as she approached. The moonstone in her headband pulsed gently and her limbs lightened, coursing with energy, the higher they climbed. It grew hotter as they wound around the path to the summit until they emerged onto the hilltop where the heat, noise and music took their breath away.

Greetings were exchanged, the tribe following Fern as she sought out the traders Nia had recommended. As she had yet to find the Weighmaster, negotiations for salt and seed were done with the goods they carried. New connections were formed with those seeking cloth as they admired the work done by the women on the Tall Folk's looms.

"Our own weaving house is built," said Belle, "We will work through the winter to make cloth for you."

Fern smiled as she left Belle to her trading, proud of the woman's confidence even though no looms had been constructed. She bid the tribe leave her, to purchase gifts and food of their own and told Rowan to use the mittens to trade with. She ran off happily with Belle and Bramble leaving Fern and Adalwin to seek out the Weighmaster.

The Standing Stone – The Gathering

The Weighmaster's tent was set at one end of the Gathering with a sheer drop behind it and men on guard all around the entrance. As Fern and Adalwin approached, they were challenged by a large hairy man with a patch over one eye but once he knew Fern came from Nia's tribe, he bowed to her and asked if she would wait while he approached the Weighmaster on her behalf.

The tent was large but dark as only the front flap was open. Candles hung in lanterns from the roof filling the interior with the smell of burnt fat as Fern approached the Weighmaster's table. He was a broad man, fair skinned like Adalwin but where his hair was golden yellow, bright red hair rose from the Weighmaster's scalp in matted dreads before falling beyond his shoulders. A slight man with a black bristly beard stood behind his high backed chair, a gifted translator who gave the Weighmaster the ability to trade with every tribe of the land.

Fern and Adalwin bowed a few paces from the table and Fern walked forward on her own.

"Greetings, Weighmaster," she said, "I bring the blessings of the goddess from Nia and her sadness that she cannot be here before you."

The translator spoke softly but quickly and the Weighmaster nodded. "I hear she is unwell."

"She fell, sir, while a storm poured from the sky and it was hours before we found her. She is recovering but was not well enough to travel."

"And you have something for me to weigh?"

"I do, sir," said Fern, reaching into the bag across her body and drawing out the gold nugget. She heard Adalwin gasp behind her and though the Weighmaster's face did not change, his translator's mouth fell open in awe.

"Our village is growing," said Fern, "We need to buy more sheep and two rams, as well as extra seed and grain. We ask your judgement on the weight and worth of my metal."

On the desk, the Weighmaster gathered weights and set them on one side of his scales before taking the nugget from Fern and placing it in the other pan. More weights were added but the scales did not move. From beneath the table, the Weighmaster placed a metal bar on the scales and they lifted the gold a tiny amount but only with the addition of a second metal bar, did the Weighmaster balance the scales.

The Weighmaster sat back in his seat, his hands on the table, his fingers tapping as he looked at the scales.

"Where did you get this gold?"

"I spoke to the goddess about our need for more animals and grain and she led me to a place in the river where I found it."

"And what says Nia about the worth of this gold?"

"She says that you will advise us of the gold's worth and it will secure us what we need."

"She is right but also wrong," said the Weighmaster. "This gold is worth what you seek but much more. No one, not even I, can make change to give you back once you've secured your purchases. This gold could buy you

10,000 sheep and 10,000 horses. You cannot use it here."

Fern looked at Adalwin whose eyes were still fixed on the gold in the pan. "What shall we do?"

The Weighmaster stood, taking the nugget from the pan.

"Take this," he insisted, "And show no one. Wilson will not speak of this and neither will I."

"But what about the sheep for the village?" asked Fern as she tucked the treasure in her bag, "How will I feed my people without them?"

The Weighmaster put his arm on her shoulder and spoke quietly. "I will secure the goods you seek in my name, with guarantee of payment from me. There are herbs Nia knows that will benefit me and my tribe and I hear your women are making good cloth. You will pay me next year, Fern with all the goods I ask for."

"And the gold?"

"Only the Weighmaster of The Circle of Circles can weigh such an amount and deliver to you its worth in such a way that you can use it. You would need to set off now if you wish to see him this year as The Circle is a day's walk away but I suggest you take up my offer, go back with your people and return early next year."

"You are wise and kind and gracious to suggest such an offer," said Fern, "And I accept and give you my promise of recompense."

"It was never in doubt," said the Weighmaster, his grey green eyes almost lost in the folds of skin which crinkled round his eyes when he smiled. "I am happy to help the tribe of Nia and Fern. Wilson, you will accompany us to Mardrake and we will secure the sheep. Whose seed looks good?"

"I spoke to Henderson," said Fern, "and Capon has agreed salt now and to deliver more by boat after harvest."

"Good choices all," nodded the Weighmaster, "Nia has taught you well. Come, let us go. The sun cooks us as we talk."

Once the deals were made, Fern and Adalwin walked through the Gathering, hand in hand. Though her cape made her sweat, it was important to represent the tribe before all these people so Fern wore it on one shoulder or the other, as they wandered among the stalls and traders. Men juggled brightly coloured bags of beans while a small dog danced on his back legs to a violin. Children squealed and shrieked as a puppeteer danced a huge furry spider towards them and men tried to throw a sack of bones the furthest, cheered on by the women. Stalls bedecked with ribbons and shells for sale swayed and tinkled in the gentle breeze.

Adalwin produced a packet of cloth strips, sewn with patterns to be used as cuffs or collars. He traded one strip for roast meat, which they ate with their fingers from a large furry leaf, and beer to drink. Fern sat at his bidding while he disappeared into the crowds of people.

The fire on the edge of the hilltop, furthest from the Weighmaster's tent, was piled high and ready to be lit and Fern watched as women helped their children tie favours on a stick and add it to the kindling. As the sun passed its zenith, dealing was almost over as people returned to their tents and horses, making ready for the evening celebrations. Fern shut her eyes to the heat and noise for a second and found it hard to reopen them. As if a bottle of sleep had been emptied over her, she caught her head nodding to the side and opened her eyes with a start. She rubbed her face, sweat stinging her eyes as Adalwin emerged from the crowd.

"Come," he said.

At the bottom of the hill, rather than walking to their tent, Adalwin led her in the opposite direction and they skirted even more of the hill's circumference before walking towards a patch of trees. The sound of water greeted Fern's ears and she ran laughing ahead of Adalwin. He caught up with her as they zigzagged between the trees, before climbing down to the riverbank. It was a perfect place to wash and they were soon naked, sitting in the shallow pool made by the wide bend in the river.

Fern lay back, her head resting on a rock as the water flowed around her, washing away her tiredness and her worries, floating her hair from her head like a basket of black snakes. She shut her eyes, luxuriating in the cool clean river until she sensed movement beside her. Her stomach flipped as she opened her eyes to Adalwin and she rolled over into his arms. He kissed her, full and hard on the lips before pushing her from him and lowering her back with her head on the stone. From a pouch at his waist he brought out a stoppered clay bottle and taking the stopper in his teeth, he poured a few drops of the contents into the palm of his hand. The sweet rich flowery smell made Fern sit up but he pushed her back and with both hands, he washed her hair. He picked out grass and mud, all the while rubbing and massaging her scalp while Fern squirmed, surprised that pressure on her head could cause such feelings between her legs.

He took her in his arms and carried her deeper into the river, holding her in its stream as the water rinsed her hair. She looked up from her river bath into his kind face, concentrated on freeing the last of her tangles. In one strong movement, he lifted her from the water and sat her legs on either side of him and then lowered her gently onto his lap. As he filled her, every sense in her body already heightened, she cried out with pleasure before his mouth found hers and she matched his rhythm as he filled her with his love.

As they dressed beside the water, Adalwin presented her with a different bottle, even smaller than the first and she carefully unstoppered it. The pungent perfume filled the air as she placed a finger on the bottle and tipped it up. She sat a moment with her finger raised, her eyes locked with Adalwin's before she rested her finger between her breasts and smeared the oil onto her skin. She heard Adalwin's sigh and blushed at the reaction she had caused. Smells both sharp and musky rose from her chest as the scent enveloped her in its exotic perfume.

As they walked together that evening around the path to the hilltop, though the track was crowded with laughing

The Standing Stone – The Gathering

people, Fern was alone in the world with Adalwin. She had led her people from their home to the Gathering, dealt and traded and had an audience with the Weighmaster. Rowan was happy with Belle and Bramble and she bid the goddess, for the hundredth time that day, to watch over the village and look after Nia. This was her time to be Fern, the young woman she really was, daughter of her tribe and Adalwin's woman. She wore her scented hair loose, tendrils held from her face by the willow frame she had made, wound round with sage and daisies. She had tied her moonstone headband around her arm. She no longer wore Nia's cape of fur but a skin one of her own, edged with fur scraps and hung with her treasures of shells, nuts and stones. Few people stepped from her path or bowed as she walked and she smiled at the thought that being herself was such a good disguise. As they walked the final two turns of the hill, they could hear the drums beginning and hurried their pace, as did the people around them.

The crowd on the hilltop stood ten deep around the fire and they could hear the Firemaster calling the gods, brandishing his flaming torch as the sun began to sink towards the horizon. Sunlight glossed the land with lilacs, pinks and golds as the Firemaster lit the edges of the ritual fire. Fingers of magenta reached out from the sun, igniting the hilltops as the ritual fire took hold and flames of orange and yellow streaked up to the sky. The crowd roared and the drummers began. Clay jars were passed and Fern took sips of beer and mead before Adalwin pulled her to him and the dancing began. They clung together as around them, men and women bumped and rubbed together. Fingers, tongues and lips sought pleasure as the heat grew and the excitement heightened.

As the fire crept to the top of the pile, a drum beat began behind Candy, quick, loud and insistent. The drummers walked towards the fire, making a path for those that followed. Carried aloft on seats, waving to the people with gold rings sparkling on their fingers, rode Mara and Adalbern. Fern clung to Adalwin's arm as they watched the procession bring the seated figures to the fire, where they alighted, still waving to the cheering people. Four jugs of beer were presented to the crowd who cheered even louder as the Firemaster tended to his charge and brought the whole fire blazing.

Adalbern, leading Mara by the hand, walked around the edge of the circle of fire, never once taking his eyes from her face while Mara flipped back her cape, revealing her naked body, painted and adorned. Fern looked up at Adalwin.

He looked into her eyes and then bent to her ear. "He makes me sick of my stomach, my own father. To show my woman as if she is a prize to be stared at is disgusting to me. You are Adalwin's woman, beautiful in all ways to me."

"I know, I know," said Fern, grabbing his face and bringing his lips to hers.

Adalbern shouted to the crowd and Mara held his hand aloft as he spoke. Most of the people didn't understand his words but those that did, passed them on. Adalwin shook his head.

"He announces that his tribe and hers will be joined by their union and that together, they will bring wealth to the people. He speaks to the crowd and calls them 'my people', as if he is king over them all. I don't want to hear this."

He turned and walked away.

"Adalwin! Wait!"

Fern caught up to him and wrapped her arms around his waist, coaxing him around to one side of the fire, away from Adalbern and Mara.

"We need not listen but I don't want to leave yet. Please stay and be here with me."

The crowd was five deep around this side of the fire so they couldn't hear Adalbern's words until a cry was taken up by the people.

"Adalwin! Adalwin!"

The crowd parted as Adalwin and Fern walked towards the fire. The Firemaster had drawn it in so it only covered half its original base. The flames burned hotter but not so high so Fern could make out but not understand the figures on the opposite side of the fire.

"My father talks of a binding between them. My own father is bewitched by a brazen slut!"

"Why did he call for you?"

"To witness his decision and for me to call her 'mother.'"

"No! Leave now, come on. You don't have to be part of this."

As the final word's left Fern's mouth the drummers began a beat which quickly grew louder and faster.

Movement and shouts on the other side of the fire suggested Mara had removed her cloak and before they could move, Fern and Adalwin saw two silhouettes leaping the fire towards them.

In that moment, they joined hands, looked into each others' eyes and leapt across the fire, away from the jumpers.

The Standing Stone – The Gathering

Acknowledgements

This book was inspired by Silbury Hill, the greatest neolithic monument in Europe whose use remains a mystery to this day. The area surrounding Silbury Hill encompasses other sites of special interest, including Avebury, West Kennett Long Barrow and The Temple at the beginning of the stone avenue at Avebury. The effort, dedication and love bestowed on the Land by our ancestors is evident to people on the earth, whatever time they live upon it.

Thank you Peter Jones, writer, formatting hero and true friend.

Thank you Ed, cover designer supreme and ideas man.

Thank you Mike, my life partner, whose belief in my stories has never waned. Thank you for listening to my words and ideas as they flowed from my pen and for supporting me while I follow my path.

Thank you for reading The Standing Stone book series, inspired by real women across the world.

Printed in Great Britain
by Amazon